Chronicles

Crimson Blade

Chronicles

Crimson Blade

Author

Daniel John Clatworthy

Editor

Philip Aldous

Publisher

Daniel Clatworthy

Proof Reader

Njål Sand

Book Logo

Scott Lee

Cover Art

Yesenia Wallace

Year of Publication

I dedicate this book to everyone that has ever helped those in need. Those that have helped others without question or cause.

It's because of the kindness of others that I was able to publish this book.

When the world around us says "No." all of you said "Yes."

Contents

In the beginning there was the Boundless and from there came the Goddesses and they set forth and brought life to the world giving it lush forests and flowing streams, bringing life to the world and there rose sentient races and they called the world Aria. Departing soon after the Goddesses left behind relics containing their power if the world ever needed them they could call upon them and as they watched from their realm in awe as the races of the world came together until one day when the love of two Goddesses created a being of unfathomable power.

Soon this being gained sentience above all others and created two races of untold power. The first he named Angelic's for their pure souls, flowing blonde hair, blue-eyes, soft skin, and wide outstretched feathered wings. The other he called Demonic's for their blackened armor like bodies, that illuminate a crimson red from among their cracks and the leather like wings that can protrude from their bodies.

The being then forced them to fight for him and his amusement and began to feed off their strife for centuries. The Goddesses watched in horror as these new races fought, but were unable to intervene due to the being's presence. Until one fateful day two from the race of Angelic's race and two from the race of Demonic's race took a stand against this being in a desperate struggle to stop the war he created. The four valiant heroes fought back against him and using a piece of the emerald-green stone called Amersion they were able to manifest their will into a power that sealed the being away in a monolith.

With the being sealed away the races took to living on Aria and the war ended. Those who fell in love took mortal form and became known as humans from that day forward. Now years have passed and the Goddesses still watch the world and the races that inhabit it. But even to them the future is unclear and little do they know what the future holds in store for them.

Chapter One

The Journey

Laying here in my bed, I look over and see the light peek though my curtains. Grabbing my pillow, I try to go back to sleep, when I hear a loud slam at the opening to my chamber. Suddenly, my bed begins to shake. I try to pretend I'm still asleep but to no avail. My friend Selph is crawling up onto my bed.

She throws off my pillow and I can see a joyous look upon her face as she lies down next to me. With a huge smile she leans over me, her brown hair caressing her cheeks as she looks down at me with her gentle brown eyes.

"Do you know what today is Drac?" she asks. "It's your eighteenth birthday! You can finally go on the grand adventure you've talked about ever since you were a child!"

I throw the bed sheets over my head and try to go back to sleep, when I hear the maids coming in from the hall. Suddenly, I'm pulled from my bed, as the maids begin to remove my pajamas. As Selph begins to whistle, one of the maids pulls over my changing screen so she can't watch as Selph lets out a regretful sigh.

"Not too rough ladies! Please, let me do this myself," I shout, as I try to break free of their death grip. One of the maids tightens the belt around my waist. Isabel, the head maid, enters and drags Selph kicking and screaming from my room. Selph cries out how it's not fair, and she tells Selph to get back to work.

As Selph leaves the room, she shouts out to me to meet her in the garden by the usual spot, before I leave on my big adventure today. I agree to and she closes the door behind her. The maids soon finish dressing me and leave the room without saying a word. How tired I am of them. I'm the Prince of an entire country! I should be allowed to sleep in, especially on my birthday.

There's a knock on my door and Borus walks in, with a big smile on his old face. He's wearing his usual black robes, with his hood on today. I ask him why and he tells me he's in mourning because one of his best friends is leaving today. I laugh, pull his hood down over his eyes and tell him he looks like an idiot.

As he lowers his hood, his flowing silver hair falls to his shoulders, and sits himself down on the edge of my bed. We sit for a few minutes, laughing and joking about the usual things. But the conversation soon takes a serious turn. He reminds me of the importance of the day, goes to my dresser and picks up the necklace that my mother used to wear.-He ties it around my neck.

It's a small green bead made of amersion. Inside the stone, there's a golden shape. Borus always joked that it looks like the head of a dragon, but I always thought it looked more like a cat. Borus leads me down the stairs, heading down towards the armory. Baron is there to greet me, and hands me something wrapped in sackcloth. He instructs me to open it. As I do, the weight of the object becomes apparent to me. It's large, but surprisingly light- it feels as if it weighs nothing.

It's a sheath, but I can't understand why he's given it to me. Baron tells me that my father had it made especially for me, for this day. The heir to the throne must travel the world for a year, to learn how to become a better King, so that when the time comes, he'll know how to serve the people he's sworn to protect. "That Sheath you have their Drac, is comprised of both steel and amersion, and it'll house the sword of the country- the Sword of Zara."

As he helps me strap the sheath to my back, ready to place a sword within it, Baron begins rambling about finding the material for this sheath; how it was a journey in itself, and how it took months of preparation just to get the design right, as he wanted nothing but the best for me. I thank both of my friends, and as I head out, in the corner of my eye, I swear I saw a tear fall from Baron's eye.

Borus and I walk down the corridors of the castle. The sound of the maids sweeping in the distance tells me they're preparing for something big. Noticing a big stain on the blue rug, Borus shouts for a maid to come and clean it. At times, I wish they wouldn't take things so seriously- a stain's a stain, and it doesn't really bother me all that much.

Borus glances at me and tells me not to worry about the upkeep of the castle. He'll see everything gets done while I'm away. That's not what I'm worried about. He should relax more before he has a heart attack.

I sigh heavily as we continue onwards, taking a quick detour through the kitchen. Borus tries to grab a quick snack, but his hand's smacked away by Isabel. I laugh as he calls her an old hag and she hits him in the head with a wooden spoon, chasing him out of the kitchen. He turns back and yells "Stingy!" as a passing shot, and then he's gone.

I leave Isabel to her work, and catch up with Borus further up the corridor. Deciding there's no more time for detours, we head out towards the gardens. A cool breeze begins to rustle the trees. I always loved coming out to the garden. Its serene beauty, the bright colors of the plants and the rushing of the water from the fountain- it always feels so alive.

In the distance, I can see the beautiful Blossom trees dropping their petals onto the ground. The two trees growing around each other are in perfect harmony. As we draw nearer to the trees, I see my father there waiting for me.

"Sire Borus" he calls out. My father walks towards us, arms spread wide, and with a smile, he embraces me. Borus tells the King that we shouldn't dilly dally- we're on a tight schedule due to the weather. I don't understand what Borus means, but I figure it's for the best that I wait and find out.

My father lets go of me, though the smell of his cologne does not. It's as if his royal mantle and beard have been soaked in it, as well as his tunic. Gagging for a brief moment, I almost don't hear him, as he instructs me to follow him to what I've always assumed are some catacombs.
Borus and my father each take hold of a handle on either side of the door and begin to pull. As a gust of wind blows against my face, a slight feeling of fear grips me. Borus looks back at me and laughs, telling me not to be afraid as he proceeds down the stairs, with me following close behind him and my father behind me.

We continue to walk down a spiral staircase, the white stone of the room smoothed to a fine finish. Borus is carrying a flaming torch in one hand, to light our way- I can see the light from the fire reflected back in his eyes. After a few minutes, we pass a massive door that had been bolted shut, with chains set into the wall to hold it shut. I try to peek through a hatch in the front, but as I stare into it my father places a hand on my back, making me jump in fright.

Borus laughs and continues down the stairs, so I follow after him, leaving the curious door behind. I wonder what was sealed away back there- what could possibly require such heavy protection? And were the locks there to keep it from being raided, or to stop something from breaking free?

"The Kingdom's greatest fear." Borus voices floats back to me, answering my thoughts. "Ever since the War of Heaven's Fall, it's been sleeping. Your ancestors took it upon themselves to lock it away, in case it ever awoke. "

I turn to my father and he shrugs. Not even he knows what's behind the door. I'm curious as to how Borus knows, but when I ask, he just laughs. He tells me he's much older than he looks, to which I ask if he is over a thousand years old. I replies that he is actually nine thousand seven hundred and fifty three years old.

Shock fills my face. My father has the same look. Borus begins to laugh uncontrollably. When the laughter finally stops, he tells us that he was joking about his age, wiping a tear from his eye as he does so.

We continue down the stairs, until Borus blows out the fire in his hand, and leaves us in the dark. For a moment, I'm overcome by a feeling of panic, but then the room begins to glow pale blue. A giant door appears on the wall before us.

I suddenly realize that the entire door is made of amersion, as is the wall surrounding the door. I watch in awe, as bright gold lettering appears upon the door in a language I-don't understand, and the door opens before us. Bright light shines out from the doors, momentarily blinding me. When I open my eyes, a giant field of flowers is laid out in front of me, stretching as far as the eye can see.

Following after Borus and my father, I take a hesitant step into the lush garden- it feels incredibly soft underfoot after the hard stone floors of the catacombs. I see a large tree in the distance, and feel the sun's warmth on the back of my neck. I look up, and sure enough, a golden orb is hanging in the sky, to light the room.

Staring off into the sky, I can't help but be amazed at what I'm witnessing- it's as if there's another world right under the castle. I see bugs pollinating flowers, I hear birds chirping in the tree, and I can smell the flowers all around me. The heat of the sun on my back overcomes me with joy and happiness, but when I look back at the entrance to the room, I'm reminded of the reality that awaits me outside.

Borus and my father are now sitting under the tree resting, talking about what my father refers to as "the best days of his life." They stop suddenly as I approach- I heard him talking about my mother, and how they came here all the time when they were younger.

My father gets to his feet, and stands before a pedestal. A sword has been driven into it, right up to the hilt. He instructs me to pull the sword from the pedestal. Borus gets up, wiping grass from his robes. Grumbling about his "tired old legs," he asks my father for five more minutes.

"Deal with it, old-timer," my Father responds, with a chuckle. "I'm not that much younger than you, and you don't see me complaining." He looks at me once more, the serious expression returning to his face. My father tells me that this sword is the sacred relic of Zarian, the weapon passed down by our ancestors from before the War of Heaven's Fall. This was one of the swords used to fight against the evil that threatened to destroy this world, and has since been used as a tool to protect the people of Zarian.

Borus tells me that it is a sacred relic, and should be treated as such, using it only when I need to. I should always look for a solution other than violence to solve my problems.

I try to take hold of what Borus is telling me as I approach the pedestal and place my hand upon the sword. I feel a sudden jolt of energy flow through my body. A ghostly apparition of a woman fades into view before me. Her hair is blonde, and her eyes sparkle with blue light; she is dressed from head to toe in a flowing white gown. She smiles at me, and bows her head before vanishing as suddenly as she appeared.

My father and Borus look at me strangely, but they say nothing to me. A few moments pass as I stand there, with one hand still resting on the hilt of the sword. Borus asks me if I'm feeling okay. Neither he, nor my father had seen the lady appear before me. I nod my head slowly and tell them of the woman that revealed herself to me. Shock filled their eyes, and they looked at one another, faces no longer bearing a trace of the jovial nature that had been there before.

Borus grabs my arms, asking me to describe the woman to him, and I do so, although his odd reaction is beginning to scare me. He lets go of me, apologizing for his outburst, saying that he shouldn't have treated me that way. I look at my father, and ask him what's wrong with Borus. He tells me that when he first laid hands on the sword, in his youth, he saw no apparition. He goes on to tell me that, as far as he was aware, no one in our family line ever seen such an apparition until now.

I take a deep breath and pull the sword from the pedestal. The world around me begins to fade away; as the light in the room fades, I place the sword in the sheath on my back. As the room fills with darkness, the sheath begins to glow a pale blue light, as if it were trying to illuminate the path and guide us out.

The three of us find the stairs in the darkness by following the light from my sheath. We head back through the catacombs, climbing higher and higher up the stairs, back towards the entrance. After being outside in the beautiful garden room, the air in here seems incredibly stale and musty. We reach the heavy black door from earlier, and I feel the sword rattle slightly inside its sheath. I dismiss those thoughts; if my father and Borus could read my mind, how crazy would they think I sound.

As we reach the top of the stairs, the light from outside shines through the open door, down into the opening of the catacombs. The light from my sheath begins to dissipate, and I distantly hear a familiar voice calling my name. Borus lets out exasperated sigh. "That girl will never give up on you." My father laughs, and I realize who the familiar voice calling out to me belongs to- it's Selph, and she's probably been waiting for me for a long time.

The moment we exit the catacombs, she is on me, pouncing like a lioness, with open arms to hold me close. I blush and try to get her off of me- I don't want my father seeing me being cuddled like this. He just laughs, and tells me to go relax. Preparations for my departure wouldn't be completed for a while yet.

I ask her how she's doing. She tells me that Isabel's still trying to get her to clean up a spill on the rug in one of the halls. She ran out here to get away from her nagging. We walk around the garden for a long while, chatting about what happened down in the catacombs. I draw the sword, to show her the legendary blade that I now possessed, but as I hold it before me now, I see the sword has changed.

It looks totally different now- the blade of the sword remained the same but an inlay had now appeared in the same text the door was in. It's a language that I don't understand. Around the inlay, the sword has become teal in color. Selph stares at the sword in amazement as do I. She asks if she can hold it, and I hand it over. As the sword leaves contact with my skin, I could've sworn that the teal tone that imbued the blade faded slightly, but as Selph held the sword aloft, attempting to look like a hero from the cover of a book she'd read, I figure I'm just imagining it.

Laughing at her silly pose, she struggles to keep the sword steady. It's too heavy for her, and she staggers to one side as she lowers it, bumping into me, giggling like a schoolgirl. The sword swings downwards and the point embeds itself in the soft turf beneath our feet. I take the sword off of her and check to make sure she hasn't dirtied the blade. It looks clean, but I wipe it with my sleeve, just to be safe. Looking at it up close, it's now beyond doubt that the sword has changed; the ornate inlay is sharp, and the teal sheen is positively glowing in my hands.

I place the sword back into its sheath, and we continue to walk through the garden. Selph tells me that she's going to miss me while I'm away on my journey, and that Isabel will probably be the death of her. I can't help but laugh at her. She asks me if I remember the day we met, when she tried to break into my room as a child and steal my necklace. I tell her I do.

"When Borus caught you, you were screaming bloody murder, crying because you thought he was either going to kill you or cut off your hands." Selph looks at me with a fierce look and tells me that I would have been the same way if I were the thief and she were the beautiful Princess.

I carry on laughing. Borus took her to Isabel, who made her a maid at the castle. "In the beginning, I honestly thought you were a no good thief- you tried to escape every chance you got. But when I was alone, missing my mother, you were the only person who sat with me and cheered me up."

She laughs, and pushes me playfully, telling me that she only stayed so she could have a crack at getting the necklace someday. But the look in her eyes tells me otherwise. Her eyes were filled with compassion and I know that she really stayed for me. I was nothing but a lonely boy wanting a friend, and I got exactly what I wanted.

In the distance, I hear the clamoring of armor. I look over Selph's shoulder to see Janto striding towards us his armor rattling as he storms over, sweat dripping from his brown hair. As he walks over to us, he grabs Selph and tells her to get back to work.

I watch as she is dragged away, yelling for me to save her. I let out a sigh, and I see her smiling back at me as Janto drags her off. I walk around the garden a little longer before I decide to lay down underneath the blossom trees.

I rest my head at the base of a tall tree filled with snow white blossom. I feel myself start to drift, and my head starts to swim. My mind takes leave of my body- I find myself in the body of another...

I watch in horror as I struggle to fight against a winged creature. It throws down a bright spear, which arcs towards me, whistling merrily as it splits the air with deadly ease. It's headed straight for me, and I won't be able to avoid it, but before it can pierce my body, a woman leaps in front of me, taking the blow square to the stomach. She falls, and I watch as she crash-lands, her blonde hair spreading about her like a halo. Smelling victory, the monster flies up close to me, going in for the kill, and I leap forward, stabbing with my sword, driving it into the creature's chest and thrusting a piece of amersion into him.

The world around me begins to shake as he lets out a tortured scream of agony. His body morphs into a transparent stone, light purple in color, and it falls to the ground with a crash. Two people walk over to me- one, a figure in black armor, and the other, a woman with silver hair. We watch as the fallen lady begins to bleed out slowly onto the rocky ground below. I can feel the bitter sting of my tears falling against my tattered clothes. -I faintly hear the elderly woman cough beside me, and tell me that everything's alright. I close my eyes, to block out the horrible image of the blonde woman smashed against the rocks, and I feel my mind start to drift once more...

I wake up in the garden...

Borus's face hovers above me as I wake, telling me that lunch is ready, and everyone is waiting for me. I pick myself up and head inside with him, until we reach the dining hall. Everyone is there- Janto wearing his finest armor, my father still dressed in the same clothes from earlier, and Selph, looking radiant in a beautiful gown. She waves me over, shouting over all the voices in the hall that she has a seat waiting for me.

Borus makes his way over to my father's side and whispers something in his ear. I hope that it isn't a surprise. I loathe surprises, but my father absolutely loves them, as do most of the servants and troops around the castle.

Taking my seat next to Selph, my father stands up and makes a toast to this auspicious occasion.

"Today is the day my son leaves on his journey. Many ancestors have longed for this day, excited about what it will bring- not only for the Kingdom but also for themselves. When I first left on my journey I was but a young boy, who knew nothing of his blood line or himself. When I turned eighteen and ventured past the castle walls, I learned many important lessons that helped guide me towards peace. And not only in this Kingdom, but the entire world too. I pray and hope that my son Drac will take heed of my words on his journey, and I pray he learns these lessons also."

I feel a bit moved listening to my father's speech, knowing that public speaking has never been easy for him. But as soon as he stops he soon starts again this time telling stories about his adventures with Janto in the Saberveen pass of Arvagi, and how he also met his dragon Ignkeal as they fought the armies of the Tri's.

As we listen to my father, Isabel walks over and places my meal down- a nice roast beast with potatoes roasted in a garlic sauce. The smell fills me with joy, as it is one of my favorite dishes. She wishes me luck on my journey before heading down the table with another plate for the guests, some of whom I know and others I have no clue who they are. At the end of the table I see a man in a sailor suit who seems out of place, but I pay little mind to it and begin to eat my meal.

As we eat and talk and my father sings drunken songs with the sailor and Borus at the end of the table, I can't help but realize that this is going to be the last time I see everyone for a long while, and as the realization sinks in I begin to eat slower.

Selph rests her hand on mine and assures me that everything will be okay, and everyone would be here waiting for me upon my return. I try to smile as I look over at her, and she leans over and gives me a hug.

Soon after we have all finished eating, my father instructs everyone to head to the castle gate for the sendoff, shouting that it's "time to send my son on his way." Selph stays by my side as we walk down the corridor. All the castle guards lined up in the hall salute as I pass, until at last, we reach the entrance of the castle.

Janto walks towards me, and stiffly wishes me luck on my journey. He hands me a pair of gauntlets, with the insignia of the Kingdom engraved upon them. He places a hand upon my shoulder, and tells me how proud he is of me- venturing out into the world on my own for the first time is a big moment in a young Prince's life. He then turns, without another word and joins the huddled mass of people stood behind me.

Borus comes to me next, and hands me a satchel. He tells me that it's enchanted with a spell. Items in the bag will leap into my hand, if my need for the item in question is great enough. I tell him thanks, but I can't help thinking to myself, that it is quite possibly the strangest enchantment I have ever heard of.

My father then walks over to me, as Borus joins the throng of people gathered to see me off. He is swaying slightly- he clearly over indulged in drink at dinner. He begins to tell me that he's procured me the finest tunic, made of the most beautiful blue fabric in all of the land, although he stops suddenly and laughs as he realizes that I'm already wearing it. Out the corner of my eye, I see Isabel grinning. The sailor interrupts my father's goodbye, patting my father on the back. "Timon!" the sailor shouts. "I got to get going! Everything is set for his departure, so take care!"

I ask my father why that sailor addressed him by his first name, and he just laughs, telling me not to worry about it. I tried to ask who he was, to which my father simply replied, "you'll know soon enough."

"Dad, were you this scared when you first left on your journey," I ask him. He lets out a big laugh. "My boy when I first left they had to get four of the castle guards to drag me to the port! But in your case, if you don't get going, Janto will take care of you for me!"

I approach my father and holding him tightly in my arms and tell him just how much I love him one last time. As I let go I wave goodbye to him, I see tears filling his eyes as I turn around and walk off into the distance.

After a while of walking down the road, the bricks underneath my feet soon vanish and they are soon replaced by dirt, and for the first time my boots begin to get dirty. I wonder if this is how adventurers feel when they're traveling seeking out dangers. I continue on my way and after a short while I begin to hear the town in the distance.

Hurriedly I continue on my way. The sounds of the town beginning to grow louder and I can barely make out sailors yelling. Suddenly the breeze blows over me wafting the unique smells of fragrances and foods towards me. The smells making me wish I had left room for a snack. Before long I find myself in front of the entrance to the town.

Two stone towers and some guardsman are before them. I overhear them telling an old woman that she cannot enter the town until her identify can be verified. Because Prince Drac will be arriving shortly and they have to make sure the area is secured.

When I reach them, they ask me for my identification. I give them a stern look, and show them the gauntlets Janto gave me. They see the insignia engraved into their steel surface. In a panic, they beg forgiveness and I begin to laugh, telling them not to worry about it. Before I leave, I tell them to let the old woman go in first, as she looks tired and exhausted.

The guardsmen continue to beg forgiveness and hurriedly open the gate to let us in. When we walk in the woman thanks me for my kindness. I tell her not to worry about it, but as I walk away, she asks me to wait a moment, saying that she wants to tell me something about my necklace.

I stop in my tracks, and slowly turn around. "Excuse me, what did you just say," I ask the elderly woman.
She walks over to me and grabs my hand, saying that I may not remember her and tells me how she used to be my caretaker after my mother passed away. She tells me that my mother and she used to be good friends, from when they lived in a small village near the Saberveen pass outside of Arvagi.

She talks about the times they would hide in the meadows and surprise travelers who were walking by. But I begin to lose control and shake her, asking about the pendant. She apologizes, and tells me that the pendant around my neck used to belong to my mother. She tells me that when she was pregnant with me, every day she would hold that pendant in her hand and pray. "Begging the Gods! Pleading with them, in the hopes that you would be different."

"She believed that the world is chaos, a mixture of light and darkness, and when she slept, she had nightmares of the chaos engulfing the world. So she prayed that you would become the answer to this world, and stop the chaos from devouring us. Then when you were born and she was took her final breath, the priests came and performed the amersion trial on you. Before her eyes, the stone turned neither black nor white, but remained neutral.

"As I held her hand in her final moments, the pendant she wore shone a bright gold and faded away, leaving only that piece of white you see now in your pendant." The woman's story moves me to tears, and I clasp my necklace in my hand. The elderly lady leans forward and kisses my forehead, and tells me to get going, and make my mother proud.

I turn to the woman and wave goodbye as I head down towards the docks. I see the sailor from earlier waving to me. He runs over and introduces himself as "The Captain" and tells me to hop onboard the ship.

As I board the boat, I notice the Captain welcoming two hooded figures onto the boat as well, but I pay little mind to it, assuming they're travelers. "Everyone on board? It's time to head on out to sea!" the Captain shouts. He continues to bark orders at the other crew members as they untie the boat and raise the mast. The sudden jolt from the wind pushing the boat knocks me over and the Captain runs to my side to pick me back up, telling me to be careful.

Heading out to sea, I can't help but feel a strong sense of adventure coming my way, with the crisp ocean air blowing against my face and the noise from the harbor fading into the distance. I wonder how long it's going to take and where we're going.

I turn to the Captain to ask him, and he tells me that it's going to take about three weeks to get to Avargi from where we are. He also tells me that it's a one way trip. I'm overcome with shock as I stumble over to the back of the boat. An entire three weeks? The Captain pats me on the back, and as he struggles not to laugh, he tells me not to worry about it. If we'd gone with my father's original plan, we would have been at sea for a month and a half!

Back at the castle, King Timon is having counsel with Borus, and Janto. He asks Borus to explain once more what he'd told them earlier. Borus repeats the story, slowly going over every last detail. While he was under the blossom tree in the garden, Drac began talking in another language, the one they refer to as the language of the Gods.

"Janto, I would appreciate it if you would trail my son on his journey" Timon requests. Janto kneels humbly before him, rises to his feet, and heads out of the room.

In the doorway, he stops for a brief moment by the balcony and grabs Selph from behind the curtain who had been eavesdropping on their conversation. Janto drags her out, ignoring Selph's protestations, as she demands to be let go, insisting that she can keep a secret. Janto looks at the King for guidance, and asks him if he can take her with him. The King agrees.

As Janto leaves the counsel, Timon asks Borus to travel to the desert of Harvgeth and check the ancient seal that his ancestors placed there. Borus agrees, kneeling and bowing his head towards the King before rising and walking out the door.

Now sitting alone in his throne, Timon looks over to his side, looking at the other throne that remains empty, wishing that his love were still with him. He prays the seal is still intact, and that all her nightmares were just that- nightmares.

Chapter Two

The Fog

A few weeks later, traversing the desert with only the footprints he leaves behind, Borus the mage stops to take a break. He gazes out across the ever expanding ocean of sand, a breeze blowing gently on his face. How much longer it would take to reach the center of the desert? He thinks back to what King Timon said.

"I'm worried about that seal. The creature that my ancestors sealed away must not be allowed to return to this realm. Please Borus, make haste and report back to me your findings."

Days pass, as Borus nears the center of the desert. Way off in the distance, a momentous building looms. It is made of crystal, and under the glow of the sun in the sky, it shone with an incandescent light, beckoning Borus to come closer.

After three days of marching, Borus reaches the tower. Standing in its shadow, an overwhelming feeling of dread washes over him. The flesh of his forearms prickles unsettlingly, and the hairs on the back of his neck begin to stand to attention. Usually always one to trust his instincts, all the signs were screaming at Borus to turn around and leave. But alas, he has a job to do, so swallowing his fear, he shoulders his heavy bag, and ventures inside.

Heading down the hall and up the stairs, he begins to climb up what feels like a never-ending flight of stairs, until he reaches the summit of the tower. In the center of the room, he sees the large transparent stone, dark purple in color. He looks over the stone, checking if for faults, and he finds none. Looking out from an opening, he loses himself in the view of the surrounding area. Walking over towards the opening and to the edge of the summit, he looks out at the view before him, fixated by its beauty.

A high, clear laugh suddenly pierces the air, echoing through his very being, followed by a bang, as if someone was knocking at the castle gates. but the room was empty. Borus then senses the enormous power radiating from the stone, drawing his eyes to it. He crosses the room automatically, unable to stop himself even though he wanted to.

Setting his gaze upon the stone, Borus lets out a moan of agony. The power radiating from the stone was resonating in the air, and a high-pitched ringing sound begins emanating through the air, rising in volume, pulsing like a siren. The feeling of his eyes burning, he sees the terrible power rising from the stone begin to materialize. It forms the shape of a shrouded figure, trapped inside the stone. It begins as nothing more than a hazy shadow, but as it slowly solidifies, it forms a solid creature, looking back at him with his hateful red eyes. He raises a fist, and strikes the stone. An odd sound marks his fist colliding with the stone; it was high and metallic, like a hammer striking an anvil in the forge.

"You know, it is only a matter of time now, man of Haven. Soon I will return and this world will fall into chaos."

His voice was the perfect vocalization of malice. As Borus examined the stone for any cracks the creature continues to laugh at him. *"You may not feel it, but the chaos in this world is feeding me even through this stone. All I needs is a little more, and nothing you or anyone in this world can do anything to stop me."*

The creature continues to stare back at Borus as if fixated on him. A noise cracks the air- a corner of the stone has been damaged, and a tiny piece chipped off. The creature cackles uncontrollably, as Borus looks up. The creature stares back at him with a smile of bright crimson red.

All of a sudden, Borus feels a jerk behind his navel, as he is lifted off of his feet. A feeling of being crushed overtakes him and he hears the voice of the creature inside his head.

"It may not be today, it may not be tomorrow but soon I will awaken and your world will at last meet its end, man of Haven. Go, tell your precious King that soon this world will be mine." As his laughter echoes through the desert, Borus is thrown from the tower. The creature's laughter fades into the distance, as the world spins out of control. All he hears is the howling of the wind, as he spirals through the air. When he crash lands on the sandy ground, he groans.

A dust cloud envelopes his body as he begins to lose consciousness.

On a ship headed to Arvagi, Janto and Selph are sat in the small, wooden cabin Selph had been given as her private quarters for the voyage.
"Okay Janto, explain this to me again."

Janto chuckles as he points down at the cards on the table. "Alright Selph, here's how it works: each card has a number on it and the symbol of your dragon. The goal is to flip the cards one by one, and place more until one of us has completed the dragon on the field."

They're playing a game of Teos, a card game generally only played by old men with too much time in their hands. It's terribly boring. Selph's eyes mist over as Janto speaks, and she looks at the cards in her hand lazily. Tuning out Janto's voice, she focuses on the pictures on the cards before her.

"Following me so far?" Selph opens her mouth to answer, but the sound of heavy boots knocking against the boat's wooden deck interrupts her before she can answer. The footsteps were hurried, and slightly uneven- without turning around, she knows who it is. It was the Captain.

"Janto, a big storm is coming, and we aren't going to avoid it. You two should actually prepare in case we need to jump ship."

"Those are bold words from an experienced sailor like yourself Captain. What makes you think we may actually need to abandon the ship?"

The Captain shifts uncomfortably on the spot, a look of uncertainty crossing his face. "Janto, Selph, please come with me." He leads them up the stairs and onto the deck of the ship. Over the bow of the ship, they see nothing but darkness, as if staring into an abyss void of all life. There are no islands in sight, and no sky up above. Just infinite darkness. And they're sailing straight into it. The Captain looks over at Janto, and sees nothing but fear in his eyes.

"You see what I mean? If this was a monster you could kill it. If it was a demon you could seal it away. This is a storm unlike any other, and no weapon will be able to cut through this. All we can do is prepare. because It's too late to turn back."

Janto stares back at the Captain and asks him. "How did this storm come to be? A sailor of your experience should have been able to avoid this!" The Captain lets out a heavy sigh. "This storm is not a natural one. We were close to the port of Arvagi but all of a sudden a giant black storm engulfed it. You can feel it too can't you, the huge demonic pressure building in the air?"

Janto looks down at his feet. "Yes, I feel it. Some great evil is working against us. I feel their ill will hanging heavy in the air around us." He turns to Selph, whose skin has turned much paler than usual. "We need to get back inside. Excuse us Captain."

As they head back to cabin, the Captain spoke. "You're planning to go and hide inside. I thought the King's men were supposed to be brave. Cowards!" Janto span on his heels, as fast as lightning. The look on his face was thunderous.

"Do not question the trustworthiness of the King. We are not hiding. We are not abandoning you. We have been sent here on an important mission. We are to follow Drac, the prince of Zaria, as he ventures forth on his noble quest. He is not to know we are here; we are the secret sword that guards him. He is here now, on this very boat, and if he were to see us, all of the King's plans would be ruined. We shall return to the cabins, and we will come back as soon as we can, disguised in a fashion that Drac won't recognize us in."

The Captain turns back to the ocean. "Very well Janto. I would hurry, the Prince has already been sent for. He shall be up on deck with us very soon." Selph grabbed Janto's arm, and tugged urgently. "There he is now. Come on."

The two of them head back inside, their faces turned away from the young prince unsteadily crossing the deck, a mere 25 yards away.

I'm looking at the gullies when the young, cabin boy comes to fetch me. He tells me that there is an emergency on deck, and the Captain has sent for me. As I climb the stairs, I hear panicked voices coming from above. I sense that something is seriously wrong; the cabin boy is beside himself with fright.

I fling open the doors, trying to look commanding and confident. It wouldn't do to have these sailors think I'm a child- I'm the Prince of Zaria. Stepping out onto the deck, I instantly notice how rough these waters feel. I'm unsteady on my feet as I cross the deck. I notice a large man dashing inside, face bowed against the sea spray. A pretty girl is with him, and I make a mental note to keep an eye out for her in the future- I was unaware that there was anyone my own age is on the boat, besides the occasional nervous cabin boy.

Looking out into the black abyss that lays before us, I listen to the waves crashing upon the ship. The noise of the Captain talking to the other passengers catches my attention, and I hurry to him. "Excuse me, Captain" I call as I reach him. "What's going on here?" The two passengers fall silent as I look them over and I stare at the Captain. "What is happening with the weather? Why are we headed directly towards it?" The Captain jumps to attention, and explains the situation. "It's too late to turn the ship back now. Our only option is to head into the eye of the storm and ride it out."

I agree with the Captain that it is the best course of action. He reassures me as we get closer to the darkness that awaits us. He begins shouting orders out and the crew begin to work frantically on the deck of the ship to prepare.

I watch, as the ship draws ever closer to the inky blackness of the storm. It looks like the darkness will simply swallow us whole. The darkness begins to slowly engulf the ship. A wave of terror overcomes

32

me, as I hear the crew scream in fright, as the entire ship is swallowed up by the darkness. I close my eyes, and wait. I've never felt so powerless in all my life.

An odd hush falls over the crew- they stop screaming as one, as though something has happened to calm their fears. I open my eyes, and the deck around me is drenched in blue light. I look around to find the source of the light, and I see the crew staring at me in shock. I look over to see the Captain also staring at me.

"Your sheath is glowing. I don't understand, what's going on here..." I take the sheath off my back and grab the hilt of my sword. The moment my hand makes contact with the hilt, a voice echoes through my mind. The sound of the wind and the waves crashing against the ship seem to fade out as it speaks, leaving just me and it alone, surrounded by the pandemonium taking place around us.

"Do not worry, Drac. This storm is not of natural origin, but I will protect you from it." As quickly as it came, the voice leaves, the sound of the ocean storm returning in full force.

I explain to the Captain what the voice had said to me. He looks at me skeptically, but he has no other choice than to trust me. He barks orders at his crew, telling them to prepare for the worst, and we continue sailing onwards through the sea. I listen to my own heartbeat thumping, and we continue to sail onwards through the sea, the incessant creaking of the ship's mast makes my heart race even faster.

Something big looms out of the darkness, illuminated by my sheath. The Captain yells to prepare for the impact, but then the figure disappears. The Captain and crew frantically look around the side of the ship for any sign of what it was. As they get closer to the edge the ship begins to shake violently. As I'm thrown to the ground, my head slamming into the deck of the ship.

I struggle to my feet, and look around, still disoriented from the fall. I can't fathom what I see. A hideous tail, scaly and blue, has reached up from the depths of the ocean, and wrapped itself around it. It looks rather like a serpent's tail, and it is clearly incredibly strong. Wood is splintering beneath its powerful grip, and cracks are spreading across the deck, threatening to throw us all into the ocean to join the scaly beast that lurks within it.

I watch as some of the crew members are crushed by the mighty creature, as more tentacles rise out of the water to join the first. Stabbing at the creature with spears, they try to fight it off, but it's scales are actually as hard as steel. The heads of the spears break as they try to piece the scales, and it continues to swing wildly, whipping men into the water, or picking them up, and throwing them down against the deck.

Watching all this, I fail to realize that the monster is wrapping itself around more of the ship and suddenly it is above me. I try to run, the churning waters and the monster mercilessly beating it, causes the boat to jerk suddenly, and I fall to the floor once more. The beast above me swings downwards with immense ferocity, looking to end me in one crushing blow. I close my eyes and pray that death comes quickly and painlessly.

A hot, metallic sound cuts the air, like a red-hot sword being struck with a hammer in a forge, and after a few seconds I open my eyes. I look up, confused. It is as if a barrier has formed in the air above me, and the beast is unable to pierce it. It strikes the barrier over and over, and each time it is repelled, with a blue flash igniting with every hit.

I look around and see two other passengers charging across the deck. They are both covered from head to toe, their faces obscured by shadows from heavy black hoods over their heads. They grab hold of me, and begin to drag me away from the splintering cracks that are crossing the deck. The deck of the ship is breaking apart and the crewmembers are beginning to fall into the sea, crashing into the dark ocean below us.

I feel the ship break apart. The screams of the crew, as they fall into the black abyss echo through my mind. Those still remaining on the splintered wreckage of the ship are frantically untying life rafts. As the ship continues sinking into the black abyss, I'm dragged to my feet by one of the hooded figures. The other grabs my wrist. The hand is small and feminine, and as they lead me towards a life raft, I wonder why these two are so interested in keeping me safe. Patriots looking to protect the Prince? Why so intent on keeping their faces covered then?

Before we can reach the life raft, the ship shakes once more. The shattered remnants of the deck are flying everywhere, and I fall to the floor once more. The smaller of the two hooded figures falls with me, still gripping my wrist, but the larger of the two remains on his feet, and tries in vein to scoop us up. There's a boom, as if a cannon has gone off nearby, and with that, he is knocked down as well. I'm thrown backwards by the sudden shake of the boat, and I land up against the other side of the ship.

I quickly look up, and I see the creature's face. It has risen out of the water, and it is staring down at me, hungrily. One of the passengers begins to pray, as the light from my sheath intensifies, revealing the creature's horrendous face to us.

Over the roar of the ocean, I hear the Captain begin to stutter. "L... L... Leviathan!" I think back to my days spent reading in the royal library. I had read many stories featuring the immortal sea creature, which guarded sacred treasures hidden on the ocean floor. They destroyed any ships that dared approach, and many a brave sea captain had been lost to the legendary monster. And now one had stepped straight out of the pages of a book, and was hovering over us, intent on pushing us into the water, and devouring us whole.

The blue light from my sheath illuminates its blue scales and its green eyes stare down at me as if trying to peer into my soul. It lets out a torturous screech, and dives into the boat. What little remains of the deck shatters apart and we are all thrown into the air. It feels as if time has slowed to a crawl. With pieces of debris falling all around me, and the two hooded passengers desperately reaching out for me, I fall into the abyss.

I feel the cold quickly envelop me. Too tired to go on, I feel myself sinking lower and lower into the sea. I feel my feet hit sand. Have I reached the bottom of the sea already? I gather my strength and swim for the surface.

I hear the screech of the Leviathan, its voice muffled and dulled by the veil of water surrounding me. The Leviathan is coming for me. Suddenly I feel something at my fingertips and I remember- the Leviathan was guarding a treasure. The numbing cold of the water has drained me of strength, but with the last of my energy, I stretch out an arm to grab the treasure buried in the sand.

As I do, bright crimson light illuminates the area around me and the water evaporates. Soaking wet and coughing, I hobble to my knees. I feel numb and exhausted, but oddly, I feel my strength returning. I look forward, and see the Leviathan. It is still charging for me, it is veering off to one side now. With a screech, it crashes into the sand and rocks in front of me.

I look down at the treasure I pulled from the ocean floor. It's another sword- this one shines with a bright red light. It has a unique overlay on it that I can hardly make out. I try to climb to my feet again, but my legs have stopped working. And in that moment, I hear a strange voice. Given the circumstances, it's remarkably friendly, but at the same time, oddly unsettling.

"Hello there. I'm impressed you're still alive. Quite a predicament you're in, eh?" I stand there, not sure what to think. Who was this person, and why can't I move? He begins to laugh. "You're trying to figure out who I am, aren't you? Ahh, no need to worry- you'll learn soon enough. For now, let's just make a deal. In exchange for borrowing your body, I'll free you from your watery grave. Unless of course, you're fine with drowning."

I think about his offer. I'm not sure I trust the disembodied voice, but with no alternative besides drowning, I agree. He sets about entering my body. I feel his mind enter mine, and the feeling is strange. It's as if my body has run away from me. I'm a passenger in my on body. It's operating of its own volition, and I have no control over its actions.

The being brushes itself off, (or rather, brushes us off) and together, we peer down into the abyss. The Leviathan is still down, struggling to get back up on its feet. I think we're going to turn and leave, but then I feel my feet leave the ground, and we begin striding towards the monster. I try to fight the being, begging him to leave the creature alone, and let us get out of here. But the being pays no attention to my wishes, and continues striding onwards, drawing closer to what must be certain doom for both of us.

As we approach the Leviathan, it screeches hatefully, and snaps at us. I'm powerless to stop the being from his insanity. It's torture- I can't even close my own eyes, to shield myself from the view of the monster as it tears us limb from limb, as it almost certainly will. Perhaps that's the being's plan: Trick the foolish boy into allowing him to take control of his body, and then jump straight into the beast's jaws, just to enjoy the experience of murder. I feel sick.

And then I hear a cold dark laugh that sends a shiver down my spine, and I realize I was right not to trust the being after all.

I hear his voice echo all around me. "You made this deal for your own survival. Now, you must live with the consequences." We leap, every fiber of my being wishing I could resist the being's control. The Leviathan snaps at us once more. Its jaws close so close to us that I feel the rush of rancid breath crashing onto our shared body. When the Leviathan opens its jaws once more, the being drops into its mouth. The monster tries to close its jaws on us once more, and we extend our arms, and grab its upper jaw, and hold it open. The Leviathan struggles to close its fangs on us. If it succeeds it will surely cut us in two, but the being seems to have imbued my body with an unnatural strength. I watch on, helpless, as he continues to hold the Leviathan's mouth open. We rise out of its mouth for leverage, and then, with minimal effort, the being throws it to the ground.

Just then I hear two splashes behind us. The being glances back, and I see the two passengers have either jumped in after me, or what little remained of the ship has finally succumbed to the power of the stormy weather. I wish I could scream at them, although I'm not sure what I would say if I could. Would I tell them to run for their lives, or would I beg for their help?

As they sink down through the water, their hoods are pulled back from their faces. The water obscures my view, but as they drop into the magical bubble of air the being summoned, I can finally see them more clearly. Befuddled I realize that the smaller and more feminine of the two is the beautiful girl I caught a glimpse of on the boat earlier. And then, I realize something even more startling. That's Selph. And the large man with her, is Janto- his long hair is dripping wet, and the look on his face could terrify even the bravest of men.

The being in my body examines them carefully, eyeing them up as Janto stares back at me. The Leviathan is lying on its side, feeble and forgotten.
"I recommend you release my friend from your grip," he says to me. I'm confused. It's as if he knows that I'm possessed. How could he? I don't look any different than I normally do. The being lets out a maniacal laugh, and asks Janto what he plans on doing if he doesn't.

Janto's eyes gleam with a black fire. Selph is looking at me fearfully. "Oh, I'll find a way to remove you, just you wait and see. And it won't necessarily be painless." Janto smiles, and draws his sword. "Well, not if I have anything to say about it anyway."

The brief conversation between the being and Janto is captivating, and Selph has been listening with a placid look on her face. I realize something is terribly wrong when I see the look slide away, to be replaced by a look of horror. The look is contagious, and spreads to Janto almost instantly. We had been so distracted by the new arrivals, that we had forgotten the Leviathan. And the bested monster had spied an opportunity to get us while our back was turned.

The Leviathan has swallowed us whole.

Panic ensues. Struggling to hold on, the being swings the crimson sword into the creatures tongue. All of a sudden, my sheath begins to glow once more, its pale blue light illuminating the slimy walls of the Leviathan's throat. The calming voice rings inside my mind once, and it tells me that everything's alright. I will be safe.

The sword must have broken the being's control over my body, and I realize I'm now in control of my body again. I've been left desperately holding onto the sword. I can hear the Leviathan screeching, and I can smell the foul odor of the Leviathan's bile below me. Looking up, I can see Janto holding onto the creature's teeth, struggling to get to me. Selph is screaming behind him. Water begins rushing in, and I hold my breath as it collides with me, cutting out all noise besides the whoosh of the water, and the screech of the Leviathan.

The Leviathan has started swimming at extreme speeds, and I can hear the sound of the ocean passing us by. For a brief moment, all things were calm. We're swimming upwards, and I'm sure that we're going to break the surface of the water in a moment. My lungs are screaming for air.

I grip the sword tighter and with an enormous crash, we're above the water. With a screech, the Leviathan spits me out, and a huge gust of air throws me upwards. In a glop of bile, saliva, and god knows what else, I crash into the ground. It's a soft and sandy beach, and I feel no pain, besides the aching of my bones. With a final screech, The Leviathan turns, and heads back out to sea, fading away into the waters of the black abyss.

I close my eyes and let go of the sword. I hear the crunch of sand under foot. Two pairs of feet- one heavy, slow and sure. The other light, fast, and graceful. It's my friends. Janto is slowly walking over to me, with Selph right behind him, listening to the ocean crash against the beach. I want to see them, to hold Selph close to me, and smell her hair as I hold her. To thank Janto for his bravery, and promise him any reward I could give. But I was too tired, too weak. I feel myself drifting, and give in, and fade off to sleep.

In every direction, all I can see are fields of wild flowers, as far as the eye can see. I struggle to figure out where I am. In the distance, I see a big tree and I walk towards it. The closer I get to it, the more clearly I can hear the voices beneath it. Two people are sat beneath the tree, laughing and talking, although I can't figure out what it is they're saying.

I've see them before they see me, and they look familiar-one is a beautiful woman, wearing a necklace that matches the one I wear around my neck. The other is dressed in older clothes. I begin running towards them, as fast as my legs will carry me, but as I do, they begin to fade into the distance. I struggle as I run towards them, stretching out my arms desperately hoping they will grab me as I fall to the ground, and with that, the world around me fades to black.

The first thing I see when I open my eyes, is Selph looking down at me. Her hair is still wet, and her eyes are red. Whether she has been crying, or the water has irritated them, I can't tell. I can feel her lap beneath my head, keeping me off the sand. As I wake, she smiles down at me, running her fingers through my hair to sweep it back from my eyes. She leans forward. "Good sleep?", she asks.

I struggle to sitting up. Janto is keeping watch over the two of us. He has lit a small fire, but it's dying down. The sun is rising in the distance, illuminating the fog over the ocean. I see him begin to wave frantically towards the ocean, and I sit up to see the Captain and the few remaining crew members rowing towards us.

I get up, and brush the sand off my pants, and help Selph up off the ground. We walk over towards the Captain. "Told the boy you've been following him I take it, Janto," the Captain calls over to us as the boat drifts towards us. Before Janto can respond to him I speak up. "I knew it was him all along, Captain. He never tried to disguise his voice. I figured my old man would send him to keep an eye on me and make sure I was safe."

Selph laughs. Janto can't hide his voice, with it's unique character being it's lack of range. He could do monotonous boredom, and confident aggression, but that was about it. We decide it would be best to rest for a bit, to allow the crew to recover their strength, and plan our next move. With no ship and no food, we have a hard journey ahead of us.

We sit around the smoldering campfire, discussing our plan of action. "If we can figure out where we are, we may be able to get directly to Arvagi from here," says the Captain. Janto, with his arms crossed, sitting down at the fire, agrees that may be a good idea but with no way of knowing where we are, it would be impossible.

I'm quietly listening to them speak, when Selph speaks up. I look at her with surprise, and she blushes slightly as she speaks. "In my youth, during my lesser days as a thief. Well... either my friends or I would always scout out houses before we robbed them. You know, make sure they don't have a dog, work out where the best escape routes are And well... although we may not be robbing anyplace right now, I think it'd be best if we sent out a scout to look around first."

The Captain and the crew agrees. As Selph has experience as a scout, we agree she should be one of those to go, and the remaining crew members all volunteer to go with her (one of whom has been sticking close to her ever since he arrived, barely tearing his eyes away from her.) After they leave, only Janto, the Captain and myself remain at the Campfire. We talk for what seems like an age about what had happened at the bottom of the ocean. A worried look appeared on the Captain's face as we regaled him with the tale. "I don't like this Janto. 'Tis as if the ocean itself... nay the world itself is trying to prevent Drac here from going forward."

As uncomfortable as it feels when people talk about me, I can't help but think this is more than just a coincidence- first a black fog engulfs the sea and then the guardian of the sea attacks our boat. Something was certainly conspiring against us. But was I the sole target of all the evil directed our way? Were the people escorting me merely being caught in the crossfire of the attempts being made on my life? If that is the case, I would rather go on alone, rather than risk my friends safety.

Across the fire, Janto rises, and fetches the sword collected from the ocean floor. In the sunlight, I can see it more clearly. It looks to be made of a strange metal, with a crimson red overlay. Engraved in it are words I can't understand. Janto looks troubled, and I can see it's an ancient weapon. Possibly even from before the war or maybe even from it.

He looks down at me as if trying to figure out the solution to a puzzle he can't understand. "Drac, Do you happen to know what this is?" I shake my head. Like him, I have no clue. It occurs to me that, when I touched the sword, I ended up being possessed. Why was this not happening to Janto?

Janto is troubled when explain to him what happened when I touched it. "That's quite strange. I do feel a demonic presence from this sword,

43

but I don't feel threatened by it." This bothers me- how could he be capable of holding a relic with such a demonic presence within it, and why couldn't I? I want to know why, and I want to know more, but before I can formulate any questions to ask Janto, Selph returns.

After letting out a deep sigh of relief, Selph sits down. She tells us that they found what they think is a village, just across a channel. I listen as the Captain lets out a hum, and scratches his chin before unbuttoning his shirt and pulling out a map that was hidden within it.

He studies the map for some time, trying to figure out where we are, when Janto chimes up. "When we were falling from Leviathan's jaw, when it spat us out on this beach, I was able to see some mountains in the distance." Suddenly, the Captain jumps to his feet, shouting "I know where we are!"

He turns the map around, and points at a tiny island. The village in the distance is the port town of Hurragath. He instructs the crew to ready the row boats. As the fire dies down we all hop in and head back out to sea.

It feels like we are on the ocean for what seems like days, slowly crossing the channel to the city on the other side. As we approach closer to Hurragath, I feel as if something is wrong. I look over to Janto, and see a serious expression on his face. I draw my arms in tightly around my body, to resist the cold chill taking hold of my body. "You feel it too?"Janto says to me, still looking off into the distance.

"It's a demonic pressure you're feeling. Whoever, or whatever created that fog... their power is emanating from that town." The Captain asks Janto what he thinks, but Janto falls silent once more.
Little by little, we approach the port. The sun is beaming down on us, and I was thinking how fair the day was, when in an instant, darkness

44

fell. It was if we had passed through an invisible barrier, which blocked out all light. Selph grabbed my arm as this happened, suddenly fearful.

The dark fog which had encased the ship earlier had returned, and it was now even thicker than before. As it had before, my sheath lit up, emanating its pale blue glow, to guide us through the fog to the port. As we get closer, the town becomes more visible. Little by little, lights in the buildings appeared out of the darkness, but the only sound we hear is the water stirring around us.

After a while we arrive at the docks, and the crew jump out first to tie the boat down. They do so quietly as they can. The cold feeling I have is growing stronger by the minute, and Janto jumps out from the boat and helps Selph and I out, as the crew helps out the Captain. Just then, we hear a loud hissing sound. The row boat has started bubbling, we watch it sink, as if the ocean swallowed it up.

I listen as Janto mumbles to himself how disheartening that was to witness. As he mumbles, the light on my sheath grew brighter extending itself around me. Selph runs over and puts her arm around mine and Janto tells me where to go. "Drac, I've been here before. It was a common place for your father and me to visit on our adventures together. We should head to the local pub- an old friend of mine runs the place, and she may know what's going on."

Walking slowly through the fog, we come across a huge tree. Janto tells us that it is the marker for the center of town. It's a giant blossom tree, much like the ones that grow back in the castle courtyard. We continue on our way, and reach the tavern. A sudden wail splits the air, and from the back of our group the Captain begins to cry. He drops to his knees.

I can't see what he's looking at, at first. It's lying on the ground, curled in a ball. As I draw nearer, the light from my sheaf illuminates the object, and I realize what it is I'm seeing. It's a body.

It takes a while to get more information out of the Captain, who is in a state of shock. We sit him down, and Selph slowly coaxes it from him. The person lying dead on the ground was his brother, a priest who looked over the city.

He pulls a small locket and a diary from his brother's pockets. The air begins to feel heavy, as we stand there watching him cry- Janto reaches his hand out and places it on the Captain's back.

The crew stands still and silent, watching their friend with tears of agony in his eyes, baring his soul before them. Minutes pass and the Captain collects himself, and pockets his brother's belongings. He points towards the tavern, and says that he needs a drink.

As we approach the tavern, we hear what sounds like scampering coming from inside. As Janto opens the tavern doors, an icicle flies by, scraping his face, and leaving a tiny cut on his cheek. I peer in through the door, and see a woman with long brown hair standing on top of the counter. She has an utterly perplexed look on her face.

Remarkably calm given the circumstances, Janto raises his hands in a signal of peace. "Hey Tina. Long time, no see! Care to let me in on what's going on around here?" The woman jumps down from the counter, and runs towards us, dragging us all inside. She slams the doors closed behind us the moment we are all in.

After making sure the doors are secured, she turns around and looks at Janto. And then, with explosive ferocity, she hits him square in the face, with what appears to be all of her strength. "A lot of good you did, you almost got us all killed, you lousy piece of shit!" she exclaims, now kicking Janto who, caught off guard by the punch, is laying on the ground.

I watch as Janto struggles to get away from Tina's barrage of kicks. I can't help but laugh, and everyone else in the room is trying to resist the temptation to join me. When she final stops, she extends her hand towards him. He coughs, clambers to his feet (unceremoniously refusing her hand) and grabs a chair. "Alright, so what did I miss exactly then, Tina?" The two begin conversing. The Captain heads behind the counter and grabs the largest bottle of whisky he can. He sits down on the floor and begins to drink.

Finding it difficult to decide what to do, Selph and I decide it's best to leave the Captain to his drinking. We sit down at the table with Janto and Tina.

Tina explains that something happened a few days ago when a Professor named Shroud was excavating an old ruined tomb of an old King. He discovered a strange artifact. Intrigued by this, he decided to study up on the artifact, and found that it possessed a dark magic. But at the time, he didn't know that.

I ask why he would even bother to study such an artifact. "Not much is known about the King that died here in Hurragath, and in the pursuit of knowledge, he wanted to know more- not only for himself but for future generations to come."

I understand the plight of knowledge, I tell her, but if he took more caution I'd assume this would have been preventable. Tina's face grows restless as I speak. '"So, can you tell me anything else, Tina?" Janto asks.

She explains that after studying the relic for a while and returning to the graveyard, a thick black fog descended and proceeded to extend itself over the island. Originally, it just covered the graveyard, but after a few days had passed, it began to grow more and more.

She continues to go on about the events that transpired explaining to us that those who ventured into the fog never came back, with the exception of the town priest, Magism, who went into the fog to get Shroud. Despite being able to rescue him, he died shortly after. His last words were "Beware the fallen King's Wrath."

We sit around the table, perplexed by her tale, when a man approaches, and sits down beside us. Slapping Janto on the back and putting an arm around Selph and myself. "Ah, so what brings you young ones here? Came for some sightseeing I take it?" he exclaims, in a loud drunken voice.

Tina drags the man over to her by his ear, and sits him down. "Janto, this is Michie. You remember him, don't you?" A puzzled look fills Janto's face as he studies the drunk man. Tina sighs deeply and moves the greasy brown hair from Michie's face to reveal tiny scar on his cheek.

Janto lets out a huge laugh, which echoes through the tavern. He explains to us that he and Michie were once sparring buddies, and that he beat him practically every time. "You see that scar he has? I put that on him when he attacked me one day. Trying to catch me off guard, because that was the only way he would ever beat me!"

Michie spits on the floor, before jumping back to his feet and demanding a rematch. He stops suddenly with a panicked look on his face, and falls to his knees. I look down to see him spewing up vile, with a smell that makes me gag.

We all think it best to go. So we rise, and leave Michie to his vomiting.

Chapter Three

Wrath

Sitting around a new table, Selph asks why the people haven't simply left the island since all the trouble started. Tina lets out a huge sigh. "Don't you remember the harbor, Selph?" I ask. She struggles to think back and her face fills with shock. "You don't mean to tell me that all the boats dissolved in the sea?"

Tina grimly nods her head, but then a thought occurs to me. "Tina, why did you bolt the door when we came inside?" Janto looks across at her with a serious expression on his face. "You really don't know do you?" she exclaims. She tells us that there have been attacks on people who venture into the fog and that they are stuck inside in the tavern.

Selph asks why the fog hasn't invaded the tavern yet. Tina explains that all the homes in the village have had wards placed upon them by Magism before his untimely demise.

We sit around the table, wondering just what we could do to get out of here, but no one has any solid ideas. Janto sits staring down at the table a worried expression filling his face. Tina tilts her head back towards the ceiling, and ponders. Selph scratches her chin, and lays her head down on the table. The only sound breaking the silence for the next few minutes, was Michie occasionally vomiting in the corner.

An idea comes to me. "We should head towards the eye of the storm." Janto turns to me, eyes widening. "That's... actually a fairly good plan!" he exclaims. Tina looks down from the ceiling once more, brow furrowed in confusion.

Janto explains to her that, if it all started from the cemetery, our best plan would be to head there. "You don't get it Janto she exclaims. The moment you step out into that fog something out there will kill you!" Tina jumps to her feet and shouts at us. But Janto calms her down, and explains that my sheath protected us from the fog and everything in it, so in theory, if we stuck close together, we should be able to navigate through the fog without trouble.

She sits back down, closes her eyes and contemplates once more. Five or so minutes pass before she finally opens her eyes. "If we're going to do this, then we need Shroud's help- he's the only person who knows who or what we're going to be facing out there."

Janto looks over at me and we both nod our heads in agreement. "For now, let's just eat. We can't do much on an empty stomach," Tina rises from her chair and heads off to the kitchen and busing herself preparing food, while Michie drags himself over to us and asks for some food too. His stomach is now entirely empty.

Janto scoots his chair over to me. He explains that this could be incredibly dangerous, and tries to talk me out of it. "Janto, I understand where you're coming from. My father asked you to protect me, but ultimately, this is my decision to make. There are people out there who need our help. Isn't this why I went on the journey in the first place?" Janto lets out a deep sigh but reluctantly agrees.

Hours pass as we walk around the tavern, stopping occasionally to talk to the towns-people who managed to escape the fog and find shelter in here. They all have stories to tell, of the screams they hear outside the walls and the scratching noises that come from the windows. But none who look out through the windows are able to report seeing anything but dense black fog.

As we continue chatting to the people, I feel the cold growing stronger, and I decide to walk over to the fireplace. The remains of a chair have been thrown on it, to keeping it burning. I wonder how many days these people have been trapped in the tavern. As I'm warming my hands, Selph joins me. She puts her cloak around my shoulders, and sits by my side.

We stare into the fire, watching the flames dance around on the wood. We watch the smaller burnt pieces, as they break off and fall into the ashes below. Selph scoots closer to me and rests her head on my shoulder. I close my eyes for a moment, but open tem again when I feel her suddenly jolt away from me. I turn to ask her what is wrong, but I stop when I see a look of shock upon her face.

I turn to see what she is looking at, only to see something in the window quickly vanish into the fog.
She yells hysterically, pointing into the darkness. Janto comes running over to quiet her. "Selph... Remain calm! We don't want to start a panic," he tells her, as he sits down by her side.

"Janto, do you think we have a chance against whatever is lurking out there in the fog?" I ask him.
"I don't know" is all he's able to say to me. The three of us sit down once more, and stare into the fire. We watch the chair slowly burn away into nothing but ashes.

A few minutes later Tina comes back from the kitchen, arms laden with some bottles of ale and a huge roasted beast. She tells everyone to gather around, and they all begin praying for thanks, despite how dark it is outside and the demonic presence in the air. I begin to feel the cold in my bones dissipating and my spirits lifting, the smell of the food luring me off the floor and to the table.

Janto and Selph soon join me at the table, and we begin talking and laughing with the town folk, about happier times. For a brief moment, we all forget the dangers outside. Our happy respite from the bleakness is interrupted however, when a huge wail is heard from outside the tavern. The moment we hear it, all thoughts of happier times, and the dinner we're consuming has just ended. Janto and I draw our swords, and the townsfolk begin picking up their dinner knives for protection. Michie staggers to his feet once more, grasping what looks like a tiny stick in his hands. I'm not sure where he got it from, but he seems convinced that he can do some damage with it.

I turn around, and see Tina putting on some torn gloves, and cracking her knuckles. The flames of the tavern begin to shake in the candles, and we all look around and nod at each other as we walk to the door. Tina looks back and tells the Captain to look after everyone. The sailors all take guard by the windows just in case.

We stand in front of the door, not knowing what to expect on the other side. Michie and Janto carefully undo the latches. As the door is thrown open, a big gust of wind blows in, knocking half the tavern's lights out. I charge out into the darkness, my sheath glowing with it's pale blue glow again, protecting all of us as we venture out.

Outside, Tina informs us that Professor Shroud is most likely still in the library, and that we should head over there. We hurry across the town, not wanting to tarry in the darkness any longer than necessary. As we venture deeper into the fog, the wailing grows louder. Passing by all the abandoned businesses, I see a flower shop, with all the flowers that were left outside now dead in their baskets. I reach out for one, and it turns to dust in my hands, falling to the ground in a shower of ash. I can hear Janto mumbling to himself behind me, asking who or what could have done such a thing.

I finally see the library through the veil of fog. We increase our pace, buoyed by the sight, when all of a sudden, a shadow runs past us at some pace. Tina raises her fists, ready to fight, and Janto, sword drawn, moves closer to me. We reach the entrance of the library, and rush to the heavy doors.

Michie begins to pound on the door, demanding that Shroud lets him in. It feels as if he is antagonizing a nest of vicious creatures with a stick. Shadows begins to surround us, as if they are trying to answer the fear that has settled in our hearts, but this time it's different- their appearance is human. A bright purple light begins to emanate from where their eyes would be, and as we focus on them, they let out a wailing sound. Their mouths become visible as they scream, emanating the same bright purple glow that came from their eyes.

The wailing brings us to our knees in pain. Michie begins fiercely banging on the door, demanding to be let in. The shadows begin to pound away on the barrier of blue light that my sheath has erected. We hear the bolts of the door clicking and sliding. When the door finally opens, we are greeted with the sight of a hooded man, his face entirely covered by shadow. The man unceremoniously grabs us, and drags us inside.

Slamming the door behind us, he bolts it shut once more. Once he's sure the door is safely secured, he slumps, and lays down against it, sweat pouring from his brow, shaking in terror. "Michie! Tina! I'm glad to see you're still alive," he mutters.

Janto helps him up off the ground, as Tina thanks Shroud for letting us in. He grabs a candle from a table, lights it and tells us to follow him. The light from my sword has died out once more, and the tiny pinprick of light from the candle is barely enough to see by. As we head through the dark halls of the library, I have to take care not to trip over the debris that is scattered everywhere.

As we head down the stairs into the cellar of the library, Shroud tells us to be careful. He tells us that this is where he's been studying since this happened. With a clunk, Selph almost loses her footing, and Tina has to grab her by the neck of her clothing, to keep her from falling head first down the stairs. Silence settles between us all, and as we examine the building going down, we see the cracks in all of the stone surfaces and a smell of mildew emanating from the cellar walls.

We reach two heavy doors, and Shroud opens them up slowly with Michie's help. We all rush into the tiny room on the other side. Shroud clears his throat, and explains that the fog outside is an ancient curse, that was embedded in a tome that he found. It's meant to absorb the life force of others to resurrect something or someone. Janto walks over to Shroud, and picks him up by the scuff of his robes.

"You're hiding something from us." Shroud looks around at everyone for help, as Janto shakes him in his hands. "Don't look at them, look at me when I am talking to you!" Tina rushes over to Janto and tries to force his hands away from Shrouds cloak. "Enough Janto," Tina exclaims "he doesn't know anything beyond that!"

As Janto lets Shroud's cloak go, Shroud struggles to catch his breath. He stands up, and tells Janto that he was right. Shock fills the room, as we listen to his story. He explains how once he had learned the spell in the tome, and what it could do, he wanted nothing more than to revive his dear deceased wife, Serina.

"Serina," Tina says in a hushed voice. Shroud tells us that he never meant for this to happen- his plan was to offer up his life in exchange for hers, so that she may live again. But when he cast the spell, something went horribly wrong.

Janto stares him down, as he continues to explain that the ritual required a sacrifice of blood, which needed to be made as the incantation was read. When he performed the spell, the wind whipped up, and Shroud's blood fell onto the blossom tree in the cemetery, instead of onto her body, failing to complete the ritual.

Michie, who is now lying up against the wall, points out that, despite the ritual being only half complete, it still did something. I listen as Shroud takes a deep breath and removes the hood of his cloak. The man standing before us is little more than a shadow. His eyes glowed purple, and his skin was half eaten away by a strange darkness.

"The ritual took what it wanted from me, but it sensed that it wasn't performed properly. It's trying to complete itself, by absorbing the life of others in the hopes it will revive what I failed to." I ask him what it was that is reviving exactly is. His glowing eyes turn to look at mine, and he tells me that the roots of the blossom tree go all the way down into all the tombs in the cemetery. They're also linked to a nearby field, where the War was fought against with the unknown King. "It is only speculation but I believe the fog is reaching out, trying to absorb the life of everyone nearby, so it can revive those fallen soldiers and townsfolk."

Dread takes hold of the room and Janto speaks up, "Shroud" he asks "do you know why those troops are dead in the fields behind Hurragath?" Shroud lifts his hood back over his head, and turns away before answering. "Yes... They were the troops of a King from a long forgotten time, during the War, all those thousands of years ago. Though the names may not be remembered, their goal of global conquest is, and it was there that the legendary Hero Dracius slayed the King and his men, to help put an end to that fight."

There's a long pause when Shroud finishes his story. Janto stares at Shroud for a good few seconds, and lets out a deep sigh "So, not only do face the threat of a fog that's slowly expanding over the sea, and probably took a good few years of life from the crew members of the ship. But we also have an army that's been dead for centuries slowly reviving that may be ready to take over the entire world. Please tell me you have some good news."

Shroud turns back around to face us once more. He explains that there is a way to momentarily stop the fog. In that brief moment when the fog has stopped, all the creatures in the fog will take physical form. If we can find the source of the failed revival and slay it, it should be possible to stop the curse.

From the back of the room, Selph asks what it will take to stop the fog. Shroud scratches his chin, looks up and tells us that he needs a sizable piece of Amersion. The only place to find a piece that's big enough, is in Magism's staff of healing.

I tell him that my Sheath is made of Amersion, but Janto who reminds me that if we use my Sheath to stop the fog, then we would have no protection against whatever is lurking outside. After a few moments of resting, Shroud scribbles down some incantations and grabs the tome from his desk and we make our way back upstairs. As we ascend, I hear Michie praying that this plan works and looking over, I see Tina with an upset look in her eyes.

We reach the entrance to the library and we begin to hear a pounding on the door. As we open it, a gust of wind once again flies past us and as we head back outside, the shadows are there, still waiting for us. My sheath once again lights up to help lead us through the fog, but suddenly we turn around to hear Shroud screaming in pain.

"It's fine!" I hear him shout. "Just continue on!" he says. Staggering along, we approach the tree and see Magism's staff. His body is missing. Shroud leans down, and smashes the wood woven around the tip of the staff to pieces and pulls the chunk of amersion from it and begins to chant the incantation he wrote down earlier in the library.

Suddenly, the fog around us begins to lift, and the sun begins to appear in the distance.
As Shroud finishes the incantation he collapses to the ground, and the barrier that surrounded us dissipates. Suddenly, screams are heard from the tavern and the townsfolk begin to come running out into the center of town with the crew following behind them.

Looking over at them, I see that the crew has begun to change like Shroud has. They have black markings covering their bodies, and their eyes are now burning a bright purple. The Captain is shouting, asking what's going on, and Janto begins trying to calm everyone down.

I remember what Shroud said- "Once the fog has lifted all the creatures will take physical form." I look around, and see piles of dust, which were left behind from where the shadows had been watching us. They begin moving, rising through the air, forming into a new shape. It takes only a few seconds for me to recognize the form they're taking, and I realize they're turning into skeletons.

I watch on in horror, as the world begins to move in slow motion. Weapons begin to form in the hands of the skeleton. They begin to slaughter the town's people in front of our eyes. The sailors struggle to fight back, but I watch as one of the skeletons plunges his hand into the chest of one of the sailors and begin to drain him of his life.

His body falls to the ground, like a piece of dried meat void of all life. As I look around, I see one skeleton coming towards me. Tina strikes it, punching its head off. It collapses to the ground.
I gain control of my senses as she shakes me. I draw my sword and begin heading towards the Captain.

As I run towards him, a skeleton turns to me and swings his sword at me. Barely ducking in time, I roll, regain my footing and strike him down. His body crumbles as I cut him down, collapsing in a shower of dust. I get close to the Captain, and I carry him inside, while the others are fighting and tell him to wait there.

I run back outside, to hear a loud clanging sound. Another Skeleton lunges at me, but is smashed to the ground by Michie, a spear in his hand. Before I can ask where he got it, he uses the hilt to dispatch another skeleton coming up from behind him.

For what feels like an eternity, we fight the skeletons. I watch as Tina shoots ice from her hands, and Janto knocks them down, sending skulls flying through the air as he beheads them. I barely avoid an attack from a large skeleton, and I strike it with my sword, turning it to ashes. As the battle rages, it becomes apparent that the skeletons are retreating. We begin to celebrate. I shout with joy, because of how excited I am that we have all survived, and as I look over at my friends

I see their joyful expressions fade.

A feeling a terror overtakes the looks on their faces, as they stare over at me and I slowly turn around to see a massive Skeleton harboring over me. I feel a sharp pain in my gut, I look down to see the point of a long sword protruding from my stomach, and blood spreading from the wound.

I look up at the Skeleton towering over me. Looking down at me, its eyes glow purple, but this one is different- there's an open flame burning brightly in his chest, the same shade of purple that glowed from their eyes. I hear its laughter, as he pulls the sword from me, and I collapse to the ground, writhing in pain.

I see crimson pouring onto the stones around me, and I start to feel light headed. I look up at the skeleton and see Janto and Michie charging at it, only to be knocked into the side of a building. Tina tries to freeze it in place, but with a single kick, it knocks her to the ground. I begin gagging on my blood, struggling to breathe. I see Shroud stand up off the ground, the creature picking him up and taking the tome from him.

"Good work Shroud. Not only have you held up your end of the bargain, but you have brought me a special sacrifice as well. The descendant of Dracius..." It occurs to me then that my ancestor fought his army and won. They would have recognized who I was by the sword I carry.

The creature lets out a boastful laugh, and leans down to me. "Do not struggle boy. Accept your death just as I did when your ancestor slayed me." I feel disgusted, knowing this is how my story ends, as my vision begins to blur. I see Shroud drop something in front of me and walk off into the distance with the creature.

I roll over, to see the sky one more time; its blue embrace is welcoming me. I can hear Janto and everyone running over, shouting at me to hold on and hang in there. As I close my eyes it feels as if eternity is passing me by. I lay there welcoming death, knowing I will soon be with my mother.

"Don't give in! If you give up the people you love will perish!" I hear a voice shouting at me. I try to look around, but I only see darkness surrounding me. Just then, an apparition appears before me, illuminating the darkness. It takes the form of a beautiful woman, with long, flowing brown hair, and green eyes. She is wearing a simple red dress. "My son, it's not your time, and you still have so much to do."

I stare at the apparition and try to call out for my mother, but all I can do is stutter. As if to answer me, she smiles, and tells me that to wake up. "I am always with you my son, even though my body is not in this world anymore. My spirit is forever by your side and in your heart. I love you."

I feel the warmth of my tears running down my cheek. I close my eyes to wipe them away and I can hear someone crying. I try to look around, but everything around me is still blurry. After a moment, my vision clears, and I realize that I'm in the tavern, lying on the floor. Selph is hovering over me, her tears falling onto my cheek.

Janto looks down at me, shock on his face. I struggle to sit up, and I look around the room, feeling a cold draft. Looking down, I see that my shirt is off and my equipment is set next to the fireplace. The wound from where I was stabbed is completely closed up. I struggle to stand up, to which Selph tells me to lay back down and that I need to rest.

Falling down to the floor, I crawl over to Janto and pull on his pants, demanding to know what happened. He looks away from me. Tina leans down, and helps me up, carrying me over to a table and sitting me down. Janto shouts out, "Don't you dare, Tina!" She silences him, shouting back "He has the right to know!"

"The right to know what?" I asked. Tina places a pendant and a diary onto the table before me. They were trinkets that the Captain took from his brother and a feeling of grief overcomes me. She explained that when Shroud left with the giant skeleton, that he dropped the incantation next to your body. But it wasn't the one that dissipated the fog. Instead, it was the one used to revive the dead.

"You were dying. There was no way we could save you. The Captain... He knew what was happening to him. He decided to do what he thought was right. With what little life he had left, he took the incantation, and despite our protests... He used the remainder of his life to save yours."

Silence falls in the room. I sit there, staring at the Captain's pendant and diary. All I can do is think of how stupid he was for giving up his life to save mine. I should have died. That should have been it for me. He threw his life away to save mine. I clench my fist in anger, and mutter to myself... "Damn fool."

Janto walks over to me and punches me clear into the wall. I struggle to get to my feet, and he picks me up, only to punch me down to the floor again. He looks at me, anger in his eyes, tears rolling down his cheek. "You're the damn fool. There was a man out there, willing to risk everything for a friend. The least you can do is honor his sacrifice!" He leans down to me to try and pick me up again, but is stopped by

Tina and Michie.

Breaking free of them, Janto storms over towards a table in a corner and stops only to grab a bottle of whisky. Tina tries to explain to me that the Captain was a good friend of his and his father's, and they traveled together a lot on my father's journey. It was why he was angry, not at me but at the loss of his friend.

For what seems like hours, we sit around the tavern, thinking of the Captain. I remember that Shroud told us that we only have a limited window of opportunity to stop the creature. I pocket the pendant and diary. I walk over towards the fireplace, and put on my tunic again and pick up my sword. "Janto, if I am to truly honor his memory, then I believe it's high time we finished the job."

Janto puts down the whisky he is drinking and picks up his sword and stares over at me, nodding his head. "Alright everyone, we don't have much time. If the fog goes up, everything we fought for will be for nothing. We have to stop that Creature, here and now! Let's teach him a lesson for taking the people we care about from us."

I lead the way through the doors of the tavern. Outside, I see more skeletons waiting for us. Lunging forward, I cut through their swords and watch as they turn to dust, not stopping to pace myself, my sword shining in the sun. I turn around and watch as Janto draws the sword that we found at the bottom of the ocean from a makeshift sheath he made, and begins to fight with both swords. The crimson sword cuts through the enemies just like mine does, but I don't stop to wonder why.

We continue to fight our way through the streets of the town. More skeletons begin to appear, climbing out from homes and windows.

Tina creates a shield of ice, blocking some of the arrows that are flying towards us. We reach the outskirts of the town, leaving the remains of our enemies in our wake. I stand on top of a hill overlooking the cemetery. A skeleton charges at me, so I quickly thrust me sword into his head and watch him turn to dust.

Looking down at the cemetery, anger fueling my every action, I see the creature from earlier staring back at me, with what can only be disgust and rage, knowing I somehow survived. We begin to run down the hill, cutting down the skeletons in our path, their blades shattering the moment they make contact with mine. I leap from the cemetery's stone wall, and plunge my sword into the creature's chest. I realize soon enough that the creature is not turning to dust like the rest, and hastily pull my sword from his chest and leap back to a safe distance. He laughs at me, "Confused, little boy? That sword will not work on me! My armies are human. I however, am a Demon." I grit my teeth, staring into his eyes. "Shroud made the mistake of trying to revive his loved one, but it backfired. The spell was only meant to revive mortal beings, not immortal beings. Your ancestor may have slain my body, but my soul remained in the Blossom tree there. So his sacrifice was able to bring back my body."

I hear my friends fighting in the background, as the creature laughs at us. I hear Janto shout out "Don't give up Drac, you can find a way!" The creature continues to laugh all of us.

"Please little mortals, do you really think you can defeat me? The one your ancestors almost died fighting! The great and mighty mad King Wrath!" He swings his sword down at me and the force of it throws me through two graves. I struggle to my feet and scream at him "I don't care who you are. You will pay with your very soul for taking the people I care about away from me!"

He quickly dashes forward, picking me up by my throat and lifting me into the air. "Then what are you going to do boy? Thanks to that fool, my body is now immortal, just like my soul. I am undead! I cannot die again." Wrath throws me into another grave, and I fall backwards as if I were a child's doll.

I shake my head, struggling to regain my senses. Wrath slowly approaches me, savoring my beating. I can feel the wound on my chest throbbing, and I stagger to my feet. He throws down his sword and I block it with mine. His maddening gaze stares me down. "Just give up and die boy! There is no way you can win! I am Immortal!"

"I will not surrender! And I won't stop until you are gone from this world. Hear me, Wrath?" I shout. I parry his sword, and he falls forward getting his weapon stuck in the blossom tree. Seizing this moment I turn and thrust my sword into Wrath' s back.

Suddenly, the world around me vanishes. Before me a blue flame appears. I look towards the flame and stare into it and it speaks back to me in a booming voice. "You who fights for your friends, what is it that you desire?" I begin to feel my body pulsing, as the flame grows stronger, and it asks me again. "You who fights for your friends, what is it that you desire?"
I clench my fists together, and stare at the blue flame. I shout "I want to protect the people I cherish in my life!" I watch as the flame engulfs the darkness around me, and the booming voice echoes. "Then do it!" I feel the world around me begin to shake and before I know it I am staring at Wraths back again.

"Hey Wrath," I exclaim, "you may have an immortal body, but your soul is far from it!" I feel the ground shaking at my feet and watch as

Wrath's body begins to crumble and turn to dust, his screams of agony echo through the cemetery. Struggling to turn around, he shouts at me, demanding to know how I have defeated him. He begins to fade away. A blue flame begins to engulf his chest, and it spreads through the rest of his body as I watch him fall to the ground. The flame continues to burn, moving onto the blossom tree where his mortal body was and finally his soul vanishes up in the remains of the blue flame.

I watch as the dust from his body gets blown away in the breeze, and I look around to see all the skeletons in the cemetery covered in blue flames, also turning to dust.

We all stop for a moment to listen, and we hear birds in the distance that begin to sing.
I take a deep breath and fall backwards onto the grass. Shroud walks over to me. "I'm sorry all this happened, it was because of my foolish attempt to revive my wife. Please, if you would end my misery?"

As I lay there staring at him, I roll back over and stare into the sky. "Sorry" I tell him. "Today, there's been way too much death for my taste. Besides, if you died, how would you atone for your sins?"
Just then, I see Janto storms over towards him. "You may not administer punishment Drac, but I damn well will!" I sit up and try to stop Janto, but it's too late.

It's as if the time is passing in slow motion, as he swings the Crimson sword from over his head with both hands towards Shroud's neck. I struggle to my feet to stop him, but as the sword grew closer and closer to killing Shroud, I close my eyes in horror. The sword stops as it touches his neck, and blood drips from the wound it leaves behind.

Janto struggles to move the sword but it has frozen in the air. Shroud speaks- not with his usual voice, but the familiar voice of the being in the sword. "Why hello again. Aren't you the one who grabbed the sword earlier from the bottom of the ocean?" Janto stands there, frozen in fear, and gawps at Shroud.

"Ah yes, and you must be the one who was using me without permission. I'm sorry but I must punish you for that." The being speaking through Shroud's body lifts up a hand and flicks Janto into big tree outside the cemetery, grabbing the sword in the blink of an eye.

"Now what do we have here? It would seem you managed to kill an immortal demon. That is quite a sight, if I do say so myself," he walks over to me. "However, I cannot allow you to put your manner of punishment onto this person you call Shroud."

I stare at the being, and it stares back at me. "You know, I just realized that we haven't even had a proper introduction, and this is the second time we've met. Allow me to introduce myself. I am Apocalypse, demon of Armageddon, but you may call me Apco if you want to."

Suddenly, the sword of Zara in my hand begins to shake fiercely, and I stare back at him, defiance in my eyes. "Hello Apco! I am Prince Drac from the Kingdom of Haven." The sword stops shaking and Apocalypse looks fiercely at me. "What did you say?" he asked me and I repeat myself. I watch as the darkness that covers Shroud's body begins to turn a crimson red, and his cloak begins to catch fire.

"Prince Drac, from the Kingdom of Haven. You are a descendant of Dracius, am I right?" he asks, eyes fixed hatefully on mine. In the corner of my eye, I see Tina and everyone else raising their weapons, and I look back over at him. "Yes. That would be the place and person alright."

In the blink of an eye, he appears before me, thrusting the crimson sword towards me. The sword of Zara jerks upwards in my hands, as if it is coming to life. It swings in the way of the blow, stopping it from connecting. Apco stands there for a moment, staring down at me. The crimson blade hovers over my sword and in that instant he vanishes. He has taken the crimson sword and the tome Shroud found with him.

Chapter Four

Debt

A breeze sweeps through the dunes of sand, and Borus wakes in a shower of sand. He's been lying still on the desert sands for the past few days. He drags himself over to the beast that carried him there, and unties its ropes. Climbing onto its back, he taps it on the side with his boot, and whispers into its ear, telling it to carry on. As Borus's blood drips from his robes he loses consciousness, and the creature continues walking, carrying Borus back the way it came through the desert.

I sit by the open window of the tavern, watching birds fly through the sky overhead, the sun hanging overhead. I can hear Tina and Janto arguing in the background. Over the few weeks we've been waiting for someone to rescue us, they've developed a bickering mother-father relationship. I find it oddly comforting. I didn't have a mother growing up, and I'm enjoying the experience of having a surrogate in the form of Tina. At that moment, they were arguing about what we should have for dinner. Selph is sitting at a table nearby, ignoring them, calmly carving away at a chunk of wood with her knife.

I look down at my lap. I'm holding the Captain's diary and I open it up to carry on reading. It was a log of my father's adventure with Janto, The Captain and a woman named Triemith. I chuckle to myself, reading a few of the passages in the book- one pertains to a small village near Arvagi, where my father and the rest managed to irritate the local bandits by trying to steal some bread from them.

I continue to turn through the pages, when a piece of paper falls out and lands on my lap. There are some strange characters scrawled across it. I can't make out what they are, but they look strangely familiar to me. I reach for my sword, and compare the writing to that on the sword. They are very similar.

Not knowing what to think of this, I place it back into the book. Hopefully, I'll figure it out someday. I go back to reading. Turning through the pages, I can't help but laugh at some of the things they all did together. I am overcome with a feeling of joy knowing that when he was my age, my father was just as naive and foolish as I sometimes am.

One passage stands out to me though as I read through.

'Journal log: day 163: Year of Stratos

Today, we snuck through Tri's territory. We came upon an ancient ruin. It looked as if it was from before the war, but that is only speculation on my part. We decided to investigate, but   what happened in there has changed our lives forever. Triemith fought and killed a strange   creature, but in doing so, was wounded badly- she lost so much blood. Timon tried to find a way to save her, but we began to lose hope. Timon picked her up and carried her into the ruins. Janto and I sat outside hoping for the best. We waited by the campfire, until we heard footsteps.   Timon and Triemith were walking together from out of the ruins. Triemith no longer looked herself- her skin was so pale, but we were just glad she was walking. We celebrated well into the night, but as we were falling asleep, I caught sight of Triemith's back as she was walking away...'

The next few pages have been torn out, as if to hide some sort of secret. I wonder if the piece of paper I saw earlier would tell me anything, but I dismiss those thoughts- I can't read what's written there anyway. For a brief moment, I consider asking Janto, but it's probably best not to pry. I know the death of the Captain was hard on him.

I take a break from reading the book, and look at the sky outside. I think of how beautiful the day is, and remember the Captain. It cost him his life of to keep me alive. I shudder as I think of the pain everyone must have felt, watching me lying there, bleeding out.

Taking hold of these thoughts, I open the journal back up and begin to read some more passages.

Journal log: day 181: Year of Stratos

Timon still seems distraught still about Triemith's leaving us. He's kept to himself these last few days. Janto and I have tried to get him to open up about what happened inside the ruins, but all he does is look at us with a sad look on his face. I know what he's going through- when I learned of my family's heritage and decided to revoke my birthright, I was the same way. We will continue to sail from Hurragath. I hope my brother will be okay staying behind there.'

I carry on skimming through, flicking through dull descriptions of mealtimes and the scenery through which they were journeying. A few pages further in, an entry catches my eye.

'Journal log: day 187: Year of Stratos

This could well be my last journal entry. Today, as we reached Ildegreath up in the mountains,   we were attacked by a small

71

platoon of Grunks. We were surrounded, and we were no match for them. Maybe Timon could have defeated them, but he surrendered instead, so that our lives would be spared. The Grunks took us through the mountains, and brought us to their   leader, King Gorsak. He wouldn't speak to us directly. He just examined us, raised his hand to his subjects, and that was it. We were picked up once more, and carried deeper down into the mountain. They threw us into a cell- three beds made of cold steel, and a stone wall with a single torch set in it for light.

If someone one day finds this journal, and reads up to this point- please, find my brother in Hurragath, and tell him that I love him. Tell him that he must fulfill the promise we made that day, all those years ago. He'll know what it means.

I turn the page, looking for the next passage, but the writing has been smudged to the point that I cannot read it. The dry ripples and calluses in the surface of the paper make me think the damage was done by tears, although I can't be certain. Hoping the next few passages will give me some solace, I continue to read, but the next round of stories seem to be about them traveling to Rigrot. I read carefully, but as nothing exciting is happening, my attention begins to wander.

I let out a deep sigh and look around the room. Selph has fallen asleep with her head on the counter, and Tina and Janto are still arguing about something. Michie is sneaking out from the back room, with what I can only assume to be a big bottle of whisky tucked under his shirt

Leaning back against the wall, I close my eyes and listen to the waves crashing against the dock, the sound of birds cutting through the noise every so often. The birds are returning to the village, now that the fog has dissipated. I hear something familiar, but also alien to me. It's the voice of someone calling out, shouting hello, and asking if anyone is out there.

I run out of the tavern, and head to the docks. A sailor is waiting for me. Janto and Tina have stopped bickering, and rushed out after me; Tina is panting heavily and Janto has a bitter look on his face. I know I can expect him to have a stern word with me later, about the dangers of running off on my own. To be fair, he'd be right in this instance- I'd even left my sword on the table inside, and if I came under attack, I'd be totally unarmed.

The Sailor begins to tell us about his journey. He claims that he's running low on supplies and asks if we could find it in our hearts to help him and his crew. Tina grabs the man, and drags him into the tavern and tells him the entire town is horribly ill with the plague and that we need a way off the island. In exchange, he can take as much as he wants for free. The sailor appears hesitant, until another sailor comes into the tavern looking for him, and he explains the deal to his comrade. The other sailor heads back to the ship to fetch the Captain, who shows up a few minutes later.

The Captain sits down at the table and introduces himself as Captain Felligrand of the Arvagi royal navy. As he does so, he tips his hat to Janto, and rudely ignores Tina, revealing himself to be a man of old-fashioned morals. Janto takes charge of negotiations, explaining the situation to him, before introducing me, shamelessly declaring that Felligrand should "watch his tongue," as he is "in the presence of the noble Prince Drac."

Before I can comment, Felligrand leaps from his chair and strides over to me. "Show me your sword boy!" he commands in a ragged voice. Not used to people speaking to me so impolitely, I'm taken aback by this man's aggression. I walk back over to my table by the window, and pick up my sword. The man takes it from me, and limps around, pacing at total random, eyes fixed upon the weapon in his hands. He turns away from me, to look across the room at Janto. "You speak some truth- he is indeed King Timon's son. But not all that leaves your tongue is honest. You're lying to me."

Janto tries to explain that he's told no lies, but seeing the way Felligrand looks at him makes him slow, and then stop his protestations. The captain storms over to Janto, and in one swift movement, strikes him down to the floor. "Boy, I've lived for almost eighty years and I can tell when a man is lying- it's kept me alive this long. Now, you'll explain to me what happened here, right now! Why are there are no people in this village! Tell me, or else I swear to the Gods, I will leave you all behind to rot."

Michie quietly crosses the room, and helps Janto up off the ground. Felligrand strides over to him. Michie winces, expecting to be the next to take a beating, but Felligrand merely shoots him a withering look, and takes the still near full whisky bottle from him. He carries the whisky over, and slams it down on the table before me. The bottle makes a dull thud when it collides with the wooden surface of the table, and I have to fight the urge to jump from the noise. Then, he steps up on a chair, and, to my surprise, climbs up onto the table. He stands there, staring down at me.

"Tell me Drac! What really happened here! And be honest with me! Your life depends on it!" I look around the room at my friends. Janto's face is swelling up badly, and Michie, Tina, and Selph are all staring back at me, unable to help me in any way. I look down, take a deep breath and begin telling Felligrand my story. I cover my fight with Wrath, and the death of the Captain, and I even cover Shroud's

74

betrayal, but I do leave out the parts of the story that involve the crimson sword, and the being that lurked within it.

When I finish telling the story, he looks down at me, keen eyes reading me, searching for the faintest sign on a lie. "Ah, honesty at last! I see you telling the truth my boy, and it makes an old sailor proud! You and your friends are welcome to come with us back to Avargi. Just help us get our ship ready and we'll set off soon."

He turns to look at Janto, and tells him that, had he been honest with him from the start, things would have gone a lot smoother. Then, with surprising grace for a man who limped so heavily the rest of the time, Felligrand hops down off the table, his threatening demeanor entirely faded away.

Felligrand gets up, taking the whisky with him and heads to the door. He pauses for a moment, and looks back at me. "You should make a grave for the Captain and his brother before we head out. A proper burial's the least they deserve! It seems you've a big debt to pay towards this 'Captain.'" Then, without saying another word, he walks out the door, leaving us to tend to Janto's wounds.

Blood is dropping from Janto's mouth, marking the floor with droplets the colour of red wine. Tina is trying to disinfect it, with a rag soaked in alcohol, but Janto is putting up an admirable fight to resist the stinging medical treatment. I head outside, to get some air, and leave them to bicker some more. I walk down the stone street, heading towards the cemetery. As I walk, Felligrand's words echo in my mind. I stop for a moment in the middle of the street, a cool breeze blowing past me. Felligrand was right- a proper burial was the least the Captain deserved, and I was going to give it to him.

I hear a door opening behind me, and I turn around. Janto is standing there, looking over at me. Without saying a word, he walks over to me, and we head towards the cemetery together. We reach the edge of the town and the ground turns to dirt. We continue on a little further, and reach the hill where the battle had raged just a few weeks before. I take a moment to look down, remembering the fight, and the chance the Captain gave us to stop this madness.

When we reach the cemetery, Janto heads into a nearby shed, emerging moments later with a pair of shovels. All the bodies that Wrath had attacked had become dust like and some have been blown away in the breeze, but we still dig anyway.

For what felt like an eternity, we keep digging. We dig plot after plot, until we have enough to represent all the townsfolk who were slain in the battle. When we have enough plots, Janto draws his sword and heads out of the cemetery. He heads to the woods nearby and begins to chop branches off the trees. I join him in this, and once we've gathered a big pile of branches we begin to make crosses for all the plots.

As the sun begins to set overhead, we place the last cross over the last plot. It's the one meant for the Captain. In the distance, I hear people approaching. I turn around and see Felligrand and his sailors walking towards us, carrying with them a few barrels. They stop and Felligrand walks over towards us. "Allow us to send his crew and these townspeople off the Arvagi way." Janto nods his head, and a few of the sailors in the back come forward with some mugs, and begin pouring rum from the barrels into each mug. I watch in surprise as instead of drinking a toast to the fallen, the sailors start pouring their mugs into each plot. Seeing my confusion, Felligrand comes over to me, and tells me that this is the most respectable way to honor a person's life in Arvagi. Each drink symbolizes the last drink that will ever have.

I pull out the diary the Captain kept, and the pendant that he had taken from his brother. I walk towards the Captain's grave, and stoop to place them into the plot. A black boot appears besides me, and gently nudges me in the side. I look up, and see Felligrand looking down at me. "Keep those lad. I'm sure he would have wanted you to have them," he tells me.

I step back, as two sailors walk over to me and Janto, and hand us the largest mugs. I look over towards Janto, and then towards Felligrand as he nods at me. We grab the mugs, and walk forward. As we pour the rum into the Captain's plot, the sailors begin to sing:

> They will always be with us,
> No matter where they are.
> The sailor men who continue
> To watch over us from afar.
>
> The brave and noble sailors ,
> Who gave their lives for a cause.
> The brave and noble sailors,
> They shall never be forgot.

As the sun sets, the sailors start lighting torches. Felligrand places a hand on my shoulder and we begin to leave one after another. The sailors continue singing until we reach the town.

We head to the port. Rowboats await us, ready to take us to Felligrand's ship. We hop in, and row across the port. The stars shine back at us from above and below, reflected back in the surface of the dark mirror of the water. No words are spoken between any of us. The crew has stopped singing and the only sound we hear as we row, is the oars breaking the surface of the water as we get closer and closer to the ship.

Chapter Five

Traitor

Tina and Michie are growing sick of sailing- Michie has been vomiting over the side of the boat nonstop for the past few weeks we've been at sea, stricken by severe seasickness. I suspect that his illness has not been aided by the copious amount of rum he has consumed since we set sail, although when I tell him so, he shrugs it off, and tells me that he's been drinking like this for his adult life, and he's too old to stop now. Tina has been watching over him, making sure he doesn't end up drunkenly leaping from the boat, or say something to one of the sailors that would lead them to throw him into the ocean, or slit his throat while sleeping.

I spend most of my days practicing my swordplay with Janto. He is a hard but a fair teacher, moving at a pace that constantly keeps me struggling to match him, but never moving so fast that I feel completely lost. He constantly critiques my footwork, calling me "a dingle berry-footed dunce." I put my weight on my heels, when I should be up on the balls of my feet like a dancer, he tells me. He says that one day someone will swing for my legs and I'll trip over on the battlefield, and impale myself on my own sword. Once, he took a swipe at my ankles, to prove his point and I did trip over my own feet trying to dodge it. I tumbled to one side and narrowly avoided crashing into Selph, who was sitting on the deck nearby, watching us.

Selph spends most of her days chatting to the sailors, who treat her like a Princess. She really seems to enjoy life at sea- she's taken to tying her hair back with a bandana like a pirate lately. Her hair's grown exponentially since we left home, and it was constantly blowing about in the wind when she stood on deck. No matter how much she said she was going to cut it, she never followed through on her claim. I'm glad- I think she looks good with her hair so long.

One morning, while I waited outside Selph's cabin while she was changing out of her nightclothes, I hear Felligrand's rough voice crying out urgently. I can't quite make out what he's saying, but when he cries out once more, I make out his words as clear as day.

"Land ho, maties!" Felligrand voice cuts through the wooden ceiling from the deck above. Land is on the horizon! That means we're almost at Arvagi! I knock on the door to Selph's room.

"Selph! Selph! Come out quick! We've arrived at Arvagi! Felligrand just said so!"

The door opens with a bang and Selph rushes out, still pulling her top on, giving me a flash of her undergarments as she does so. I'm so surprised, I blush profusely, however Selph doesn't even notice. Grabbing me by the arm and pulling me away with surprising strength. Her hair is still hanging loose, and as we climb the stairs to the deck, it flies back in my face, tickling my skin in a not so unpleasant way.

The crew is scuttling about on the deck of the ship, making preparations for our arrival at the port. Janto pulls me to the back of the boat so that I'm not in anyone's way, telling me that when we arrive we need to head into town and head to the library.

Selph drags me away from Janto, and leads me into the captain's quarters. I want to ask why she wants such secrecy so urgently, but she shushes me the moment I open my mouth.

"We know so little about the crimson sword that possessed Shroud. We don't even know why that being possessed him in the first place." She looks into my eyes with severity on her face.

I tell her that Janto had just suggested we head to the library the moment we reach the port and she agrees to come with us as well. We were in no hurry and we could take some time before we went to the castle to meet with the Queen.

There's a knock on the door, and Michie stumbles in, still rubbing sleep out of his eyes. He complains for a full minute about the sailors making so much racket, and only stops when Selph tells him that the reason they're making all that noise, is because we're preparing to dock. He instantly perks up when he hears this, and starts talking about how exciting it is to get the chance to meet the Queen.

Michie left the door slightly ajar, and I hear the hinges creak slightly as it opens up fully. I'm greeted by Tina's smiling face poking in on our conversation. She looks down at our slightly ragged outfits, laughs, and tells us that we'll have head to the tailors and get new clothes made before we visit the Queen. It wouldn't do for a Prince to been seen visiting a royal palace dressed in rags!

"You lot wouldn't be talking about me now, would you?" Felligrand's gravelly voice chimes in from the deck. He enters the room and tells us that we've docked at Arvagi and that this is where our time travelling together comes to a close.

We file out of the room and head back to the deck of the ship. As they meet, Janto gives him a stern look and extends his hand, offering his thanks for transporting us here safely. There have been few words spoken between the two of them all journey. Janto never forgave him for punching him in the face back on the island. Felligrand looks him in

81

the eye, and accepts his thanks graciously, although I think it's fair to say, he'd probably be quite content if he never saw Janto ever again. He turns to me, and with a much more sincere smile, he tells us that if we ever need an old seadog to lend us a hand, we've only to ask.

As we disembark the ship, I'm struck by the hustle and bustle of our new surroundings. After being on the ship for so long, this place seems like total pandemonium. As we head down the pier, we see hundreds of people congregated in a market square, jostling to look at the plentiful food on offer. Michie makes a beeline for a nearby fruit stall and asks for one of everything. Selph wanders off into the crowd after she spots a stall that sells newly imported knives and weaponry. Noticing the impressive gauntlets on display, Tina follows her into the crowd, leaving me with only Janto for company.

We peruse the market stalls, looking for something good to eat. One vendor tries selling us some "fresh mystery meat," but on closer inspection, the meat turns out to be a putrid shade of green and we back away cautiously. Shaking our heads at the man who was selling it.

In the end, we settle for some fresh fruit and a piece of fried dough each. We sit down on a low wall, to eat our meal, and watch the hustle and bustle going on all around us. Tina and Selph soon join us and as we eat, Tina shows off her new gauntlets, which have replaced her worn-out old gloves, and Selph is gleefully excited about the new combat knife she bought for twenty silver pieces.

Finishing our meal, Janto tells us it's time we head to the library and we head off. He says he's been to this town many times before on his adventures with my father. As we continue walking down the road, I almost trip over a rough patch of bricks, which protruded from the ground unevenly. Michie grabs a hold of me before I fall and tells me to be careful. I thank him and then bump into the back of Janto, whom stopped abruptly in front of me. He glances back at me and tells us that we've arrived.

The building is huge, with beautiful golden inlay work. It looks just like the kind of beautiful architecture I would expect to see back home at the castle. It's walls are carved from an elegant white stone, stretching up at least one hundred and fifty feet into the sky. Janto smiles at me. "If you think that is impressive, just wait till you see inside."

We head in, through the heavy oak doors, and begin to climb the stairs. It's a long climb and by the time we reach the top, we're all slightly out of breath, with the exception of Janto. We gather around the directory, and discuss what we know about the sword.

"Alright, so let's see, it's a crimson sword, that we found off the coast of Devil's Peak, guarded by the leviathan. It possessed both Drac and Shroud. The language on the sword is written in the language of the Gods from before the war. Oh, and it can teleport" Janto says.

We speculate as to what it could be, and in which section we might find text about it. We ultimately decide it's best to split up. I go with Janto, and we head to the section devoted solely for forgotten relics. "Janto, how did you know the sword was written in the language of the Gods?" I ask him

He tells me that on his journey with my father, he wanted to know what happened to one of his friends. He tried to figure it out by himself, but in the end couldn't because he was unable to translate some old text.

"You were trying to figure out what happened to Triemith?"

He stops suddenly, and looks me straight in the eye. He asks how I know about that. I tell him how I had read the Captain's diary, and he sighs deeply. He tells me that my father wouldn't disclose anything about what happened in the ruins to himself or the Captain. He wouldn't tell them what saved her life, and that the Captain and him were worried about Timon for the longest time after she left their group.

As we continue to talk, Janto and I start searching the shelves for books that might help us in our hunt for information about the crimson sword. After a few minutes of rifling through dusty old texts, I spot a thick, leather bound book on the highest shelf. Something about it draws my eye - it looks so older, and so much more ornate than all the books surrounding it. I get Janto's attention, and he tries lifting me up to reach the book, but no matter how much I stretch, I can't get more than a fingertip on its spine. A librarian walks over and asks us if we need a hand.

After a brief explanation, he heads off to fetch us a ladder. While we wait, I ask Janto what my father was like when they journeyed together. He tells me that my father was just like me, except he got into trouble more often. Then he laughs and says that we just get into dangerous situations more often

I pull out the Captain's diary and ask Janto about the paper with the God's language on it. He tells me that he didn't know what it meant, but when he confronted my father about it after the incident with Triemith, my father claimed that even he didn't know what it said. However, he did admit that whatever it said, had saved Triemith's life that day.

The librarian returns with a wooden ladder, and I'm able to climb to the top and grab the book. Hoping for some sort of clue, we gathered all the books up and headed towards the back of the library, where we could study in peace. Selph and the others were already waiting for us, and we all began scouring the books looking for some sort of clues.

For the next few hours, we read. I choose the old leather bound book – something catches my eye in the third chapter. It's a passage regarding the War of Heaven's Fall:

"Two heroes of light and two heroes of darkness fought against the chaos that threatened to engulf the world. Their bodies now mortal, they risked their lives to seal the ancient evil away using the gift of amersion. But alas with the evil defeated, the cost was high - one of the heroes lay slain on the ground.

Zara, the heroine of light, gave her life to save her love and the world. In a spout of rage, her love struck back at the others and in their defense, sealed him away. As Zara's body began to take root, she placed her soul into her sword and with a smile on her face, she faded from the world her soul sealed away and her body then turned to stone."

I tell the others of my find, and Janto takes the book and reads it intently. When he's finished, he searches for the author's name, but there doesn't seem to be one written in it anywhere. "The book's talking about after the war, not during it when your ancestors were already in mortal form. I thought there wasn't anything about that," Janto says to us.

I remember what happened in the cemetery, when something or someone was trying to tell me something. When Apocalypse tried attacking me, the Sword of Zara had acted on its own to protect me.

I explain to the others that I might know what the crimson sword is - the passage tells the story of the moment Apocalypse was sealed away inside the sword. I tell them about my sword's strange behavior, and that my sword might be the fabled Sword of Zara.

"So... You think the crimson sword contains the soul of Zara's lover, and your sword contains the soul of Zara herself?" Janto asks me. I agree, and as if to answer us, my sheath begins to glow a vibrant blue, engulfing us all in its bright light. I feel the ground jerk away from beneath me, and for a moment feel as though I'm flying.

When the light fades, we're hovering in the sky, looking down on four people. Surrounded by mountains, the little group is stood in a small clearing. For a brief moment though, I think I see someone watching them from the distance, but when I look, I can't see anyone, so I turn my attention back to the little group. They are stood around a blonde haired woman who is lying on the ground. I see a tall, dark haired man wearing tattered clothing, holding a sword in one hand and an amersion crystal in his other. Beside him there's a woman with silver hair, dressed in a similar fashion to the woman with blonde hair. The woman with the silver hair sits down beside the woman lying on the ground and takes her hands. We watch as the woman on the ground slowly bleeds out. Another man, clad in black armor turns away, tears streaming down his cheeks.

The man with the black hair walks towards the woman lying on the ground and she mutters something to him. The man lays the sword down next to her, and then raises the crystal above his head. A bright blue light engulfs them all for a brief moment and when it fades away once more, the sword is shining with its own bright blue light. The language of the Gods begins to appear, the same writing that can be seen on the Sword of Zara on my back.

As the body of the woman begins to turn to stone, the man in the black armor lets out a scream of anguish that echoes through the mountains. The mountains crack and crumble from the sound, and showers of dust slide down on the group. The silver haired woman goes over to the other man, with a sad expression filling her face.

We watch as the man in black armor, in agony at the loss of the woman, pounds his fist into the ground shattering the earth around him. He begins shouting, blaming the other two for her death. In a fit of rage, he draws his sword and charges at the man in tattered clothes.

The man barely has time to react, and just barely manages to block his attack, with the amersion crystal in his hand. The man in tattered clothes darts away, screaming at him to calm down. The man in the black armor refuses, and comes at him once more. The man in tatters tells him that he's sorry, and raises the crystal once more. A red light engulfs them and as it fades, the sword and armor the man was wearing falls to the ground.

I watch as the man in tattered clothes falls to the ground crying at the loss of two of his friends the woman leans down to comfort him her tears falling onto his back as she holds him close. Writing begins to appear across the blade lying on the ground, and I see now that it is the crimson sword that once held Apocalypse prisoner. We have just witnessed the origins of the Sword of Zara and the Crimson Sword.

The world around us fades away and a moment later, we are stood in the library once more. I open my mouth to speak, but Janto silences me. Telling me it's best we wait until we are somewhere more private before we discuss what we just saw. We head out of the library, planning to head to the shopping area, and get ourselves some new clothes. Selph slots the leather bound book into my satchel, telling me we should take it with us, so we can research it some more when the chance presents itself.

As we head down the steps outside, we're stopped by two men, dressed in ruby red coats, who claim to be ambassadors from the castle. They request that we come with them at once. Janto looks them over and I can see Tina clenching her fist in the corner of my eye.

Michie asks what they want from us, and they tell us that they wish to escort us to the castle, referring to us all by name. Michie asks them how they knew who we were, to which they explain that Felligrand had let the castle know of our arrival, and that we would most likely be found at the library.

Janto reluctantly agrees that we should go with them. We walk over towards a carriage, pulled by two giant hounds. Selph looks at the massive dogs apprehensively, and the ambassadors assure us that travel to the castle is safe, and the hounds are well trained. We climb into the carriage, and the two men instruct the driver to take us to the castle

Minutes roll past as I listen to Tina and Selph chat about the view outside, and how they can't wait to visit all the stores in town. Selph keeps commenting on how beautiful everyone's jewelry is and hopes that someday I will get her something like the people outside are wearing.

When the carriage draws to a halt, we are told to wait there for a brief moment. I poke my head out the carriage doors and I see a massive castle, comprised of dark gray stone, sitting on top of a massive cliff. There are ruby red banners flowing from the castle's windows, each one emblazoned with the Arvagi crest of a black hawk. The two ambassadors are pushing open some huge, wrought iron gates, which look and sound ancient, producing a loud creaking groan as they part.

I close the carriage door and return to my seat as we start moving again. A short while later, there's a knock on the carriage door and we hear one of the ambassadors tell us that we've arrived, opening the door after his announcement.

Janto climbs out first, followed by Michie, Tina and Selph. The two ambassadors walk over to the front doors of the castle and announce that the party from the Zarian Empire have arrived. The doors slowly open and a gust of cold air blasts past us. A man wearing a black tunic with a gold lining leads us inside. Janto walks over, and the man welcomes him to the castle. He introduces himself to me as Lord Varkus, Head of the Royal Navy of Arvagi.

He tells us that dinner will be ready momentarily, and asks that we follow him. He leads us down a long hallway that's dimly lit by torches on the walls. A long red carpet covers the floor, and the walls are made of the same dark gray stone we could see from the outside.

As we walk, Varkus tells us about the castle's heritage. He explains that when the heir to the throne comes of age they can choose to challenge the current ruler of the land to a duel to the death. If they are the victor, then they become the new ruler of the land.

I'm disgusted to hear this. I can't believe that all the Kings and Queens of the land here in Arvagi have had to kill their predecessor to become the ruler. Soon, Varkus stops at a doorway and informs us that behind this door is a room set aside for us and inside there are three beds prepared, as well as new clothes and a bath. He then walked a few feet more, and shows Selph and Tina to a room set aside for them, with new dresses and jewelry for them, compliments of the Queen.

He walks down the hall a short way before turning back, and tells us that dinner will be ready in a few hours and we should dress appropriately, as the Queen will be joining us this evening.

Varkus heads down the hall, and soon vanishes from sight. We head into our rooms.

Michie goes into the bathroom, while Janto and I sit down on our beds. I ask him why he looked so serious earlier, and he replies that he never trusts anyone who dresses fancier than he does, and I laugh.

After a while, Michie returns looking refreshed, and he tells me that there is some more bath water set aside for me and Janto. I head into the bathroom, and remove my tunic. I move my hand over the scar on my stomach that Wrath's blade left behind.

I throw my clothes into a pile on the floor, as I pour the water into the tub. Steam rises through the air from the hot water. As I slide into the water, it feels as if its warmth is soothing my very soul, and for a few minutes, I am in complete bliss.

After I've finished bathing, I hop out of the bath and drain the water. I'm drying myself off with a soft white towel, when I notice a mirror in the corner. Wiping the condensation from the mirror, I see a stranger looking back at me. I know the person in the mirror is me, but at the same time, I know it's not me. Even though it's only been a month or so since I left home, I feel as though I've changed a lot and I start to wonder what I'll look like by the time my journey's over.

I know that someday I will replace my father as the ruler of Zarian, but do I really have what it takes to be a great King. There's a knock on the door and I hear Michie yelling for me to hurry up. I take a deep breath, secure the towel around my waist, and pick my clothes from the floor.

As I walk through the door, Janto goes into the bathroom and shuts the door behind him. Michie tells me that my new clothes are on the middle bed for me. Despite being dressed by maids every morning, finally being able to do it by myself is a feeling I relish. I pull forward a folding screen around me, and put on the new pants and tunic the Queen has procured for me, along with a beautiful blue vest.

The clothes fit perfectly and I'm curious as to how they tailor knew my measurements so well. After getting dressed, I look around for my satchel and sword but they're nowhere to be found. Michie informs me that Varkus came by, and took them down to the storeroom where they will be until we leave.

This irritates me, but Janto reassures me from the bathroom that that's just how they are here. When he visited here with my father on his journey, they were told to do the same, and they were just as reluctant to part with their equipment as I am now. I lean back on my bed, callout to Janto, and ask him why he was so on edge earlier and he tells me that the King who ruled this castle before, when my father and him visited here, was ruthless, running the local town and the castle with little regard to human life.

"Perhaps the new queen is different to her predecessor," I say to Janto. He lets out a sigh, and I can tell he's just worried about our safety. I lie back, and feel my eyes grow heavy. I tell Janto that I'm going to take a nap, and ask him to wake me when it's time for dinner.

Meanwhile, Varkus is walking down a dimly lit corridor, examining the sword of Zara. Curious about the ornate blade in his hands, he draws the sword from its sheath and holds it up to the light. He senses a presence behind him, and he swings the blade down as he turns around but it's blocked by a hooded figure standing behind him with a Crimson sword. The figure laughs, and tells him that he is here to make a deal with him.

Varkus stares at the hooded figure, who lets out a small chuckle before telling Varkus the heritage of this Kingdom.

"This Kingdom is built upon the death and ruin of others. Heirs killing heirs, in a never ending struggle to become better than their predecessor. But what if the ruler of this Kingdom had no heir? Then the Kingdom would fall to their right hand subordinate. In this case, that would be you."

Varkus replies that it is treason to talk of such things, and he goes to draw the sword once again. The hooded figure shows no fear, and calmly walks over towards Varkus, placing his hand onto the hilt of the sword.

"Don't embarrass yourself. If you were going to stop me, you would have done so already. You're hesitating. You want power, instead of being the Queen's humble lap dog, and you know that I can make that happen."

Standing there, Varkus stares into the darkness of the hood, slowly moving his hand away from the sword, and the hooded figure speaks.

"What I want you to do is blame Drac for the Queen's sudden death and then collect me from the treasury in the ensuing panic. That is all you need to do and the Kingdom will be yours."

"What is it you want In return for giving me the throne?" Varkus asks. A bright crimson smile begins to illuminate the darkness under the hood before he speaks again.

"I simply want you to throw Drac into prison, and then seize the opportunity and attack the Kingdom of Haven. In this time of peace, they won't be prepared for war. They will not be able to put up a fight at all. A victory with little causalities."

A smile appears on Varkus's face as he extends his hand towards the hooded figure and agrees to the deal. The sword of Zara begins to shake ever so slightly in its sheath, as if to try and communicate in vain.

A knock of the door stirs me from my sleep, and I wake up to a woman walking into the room. Michie and Janto climb out of their beds, as she requests that we follow her. We head out of our room, and find Selph and Tina waiting for us. Both are dressed in new outfits, Tina wearing a slim black evening gown that contours to her body, and Selph is in a matching red one that looks fantastic.

The woman introduces herself as Camilla, and tells us that dinner will soon be served. She tells us to follow her and we follow her through the corridor, and up a flight of stairs, until we reach the dining hall, which is situated between two of the towers.

Looking around, I see butlers pulling out seats so that we may sit down. After we're seated, they leave the room, and I begin to wonder why the dining room is situated in such an awkward position. Before any of us can say anything, the butlers return, placing an entire roast beast with potatoes onto the table before us. My mouth begins to salivate at the smell of it. A butler offers Michie a bottle of wine and tells him it's one hundred years old.

On my left, I see Janto sitting with his arms crossed, as Camilla tries offering him a drink. He looks at her in silence. Camilla lets out a sigh and tells him not to look so awful, as the Queen will be here soon and meeting her majesty is a rare privilege. No one has seen her since she became the Queen.

Michie stops pouring the wine for a brief moment and looks over at Camilla and Janto stares back at her as well asking if she was serious, to which she tells us that she is. Camilla then pours Janto a drink and hurriedly leaves the room as a loud gong is rang and a butler says the Queen is on her way.

I watch as the rest of the butlers and Camilla scamper from the dining room, and close the doors behind them. Turning to see the doors at the far end of the room swing open, a gust of air puts out all the candles on the table. I hear footsteps approaching, and the sound of platform shoes on stone echoes around the room, until it stops suddenly and we hear someone sit down.

Staring into the darkness, I hear a yawn and a sudden snap of someone's fingers as the candles in the room light up again, burning with an ominous blue flame that lights up the entire room.
Janto suddenly gets to his feet, slamming his hands into the table as he tries to gather his words.

"Triemith" he shouts across the table. A woman with stunning black hair sits on the throne before us, in a red and black evening dress, made in a similar design to Tina and Selph's. Sitting there with a gentle smile on her face, she looks cooly over at Janto. "Long time no see Janto. How are things?'" she ask him.

Selph, Tina, Michie and I are at a loss for words. She explains to us that when she traveled with my father and Janto all those years ago she had always been a Princess of Arvagi. But upon her return to the castle, she learned that her father was dying of a rare medical condition known as Fright's disease and he begged her to take his spot on the throne.

She goes on to explain that, to fulfill the tradition of the Kingdom, she challenged him to a duel to the death, in front of his subordinates, and he stood before her and ran himself into her blade. With his final words, he thanked her for fulfilling the tradition of his ancestors.

Janto apologizes to her, and explains that he always thought the Kingdom of Arvagi was filled with nothing but brutal traditions that needed to end. She smiles, and tells us that those traditions will end with her.

She welcomes us to the castle and introduces herself to me as Queen Triemith. I stand and bow in respect to her. Janto interrupts us, asking what happened with Triemith and why she left. She then looks back at him and asks what Timon told him. Janto is very confused. "What do you mean has he told us or not?" he asks.

But before Triemith can say anything Varkus appears before us, and stabs a sword through the back of her chair, sinking his blade straight into her heart. We watch in horror as she collapses into her food.

Janto rises from his chair with lightning speed, and charges at Varkus, but he easily dodges the attack. Varkus knocks him to the ground with a swift elbow in the neck. Tina grabs the knife from the roast beast and charges at Varkus, but he lifts her up and throws her into the doors that Triemith came through.

Before I can make a move, we hear him call out for the guards, who storm into the room. Janto struggles to his feet, and Varkus kicks him against the window. He tells the other guards that we have assassinated the Queen.

He points toward the knife that Tina had and the sword in the back of her chair. Michie grabs the bottle of wine and throws it into the candles flames letting out a blinding light, and I feel someone's arm take hold of me. Glass shatters all around me.

As my sight returns, I see that it is Michie holding onto me, as we fall from the window into some tree's below. When he hit the ground, he lets go of me, and I stand up to see Tina, Selph and Janto all jumping out of the dining room after us. Varkus soon appears at the window, and looks down on us, demanding that we are caught and brought to justice for our crimes.

Janto nods to us and we all begin running towards the entrance of the castle, where we see the carriage that we took earlier. We quickly climb up onto the top of it and begin to jump down and run down the hill. The wind rushing past us, we get to the entrance of the city. Looking back towards the castle we begin to see the light of torches descending from the hill and the clamoring of troops in armor.

Janto runs over towards a low bridge, which hangs over a river that meanders through the town, and jumps over the side, onto the riverbank below. We follow after him, and hide underneath the bridge as we hear soldiers crossing the bridge into town. After a while, the noise stops. Selph turns to us and nods that it's okay. We climb back onto the bridge.

Selph tells us to stick to the shadows, and make as little noise as possible. Janto nods in agreement, and tells us that we need to make haste back to the library. Selph argues with Janto asking why the library, to which he explains we will know when we get there.

As we move off the bridge and into the shadows of the buildings, we can hear troops running back towards the bridge, asking if we've seen anyone. Varkus arrives and demands the search party spread out, and looks in every house if they need too.

When we hear this, Janto sneaks over towards us. "See what I mean now Drac? No respect for human life at all," he whispers. I see what he meant earlier. Making our way through the back alleys, Selph continues to take point, telling us when to hide when troops walk by with torches, or when they begin to break into a person's home. We hear screaming from all around town and watch in horror as flames begin to rise above the rooftops.

A feeling of disgust overwhelms me as I watch the flames grow higher into the sky. Janto grabs me and pulls me along until the flames fade from my view. After a short while, we reach the library. He instructs us to stay close to him as we all pile against the wall and we sneak past two guards stationed out front.

Once inside, we follow him to the back of the library, not far from where we were earlier. Janto begins to scour the wall as if looking for something. In the distance, the sound of armor clanking approaches us. Worrying we may have tipped off the guards, he begins to search, whispering how this would be so much easier if we still had my sheath.

Just then, we all hear a loud click and as I squint my eyes looking at Janto, I see a small opening appear next to the bookshelf. Janto tells us to follow him, and we silently scamper through the opening which closes behind us after we all make it through.

Janto breathes a heavy sigh of relief and tells us that we're safe now. Selph asks where "here" is and he explains to us that when he and my father first visited Avargi, they came to the library, to read up on demon and angelic bloodlines, hoping to learn more about what was happening to my father during his transition, when they discovered that secret passage.

Tina asks if there is a way out. Janto says yes, and it leads directly to the Saberveen pass. But before we can celebrate, torches catch light all around us and three people begin to walk forward.

Camilla appears before us, accompanied by some of the butlers from the castle. She tells us that the entire Kingdom is out looking for us. Janto asks her if she is here for a fight to which she responds that they are here following the orders they were given by the Queen. We look around at each other and I see that Janto has a serious expression on his face. The butler then approaches us.

In the torchlight, I see that his eyes are a beautiful shade of orange and his hair is jet black. He bows to me and hands me the Sword of Zara, along with my satchel. Inside, all of our equipment is gathered, including both mine and Tina's gauntlets, as well as Selph's knives and my books and our clothes all cleaned.

Another Butler comes forward, and hands Janto his equipment, and Michie his spear. Camilla tells us to be careful as by now Varkus has most likely instructed all of his men to kill us on sight, but if we continue through this tunnel, we should be able to make it to the pass in three days time.

We thank her and she hands us some rations, wrapped up in a brown package, tied shut with a simple piece of string. The butlers hand us their torches. As we put our equipment back on and get changed, Camilla and the butlers vanish into the darkness as if they were never there at all.

Chapter Six

Old Wounds

Weeks have passed as Borus now makes his way through the castle, sand falling onto the rug. Isabel begins to complain, only to silence herself when she notices the serious expression on Borus's face. Storming into the throne room he shuts the doors behind him with his presence alone and approaches the King.

Timon's face becomes one of worry and then dread as Borus's silence becomes enough to answer the Kings fears. For a short while the room remains silent until a pecking is heard on the glass on the balcony. Timon looks over to see a black bird sitting there with a note tied to its leg and he walks over opening the balcony doors.

The bird hops onto King Timon's hands and he begins to untie the note attached to its leg and begins to read it. He then crumbles the paper in his hands and tells Borus to prepare the troops for war. In shock Borus demands to know why and Timon explains the message is from "her" and that they are on their way here right now.

Borus bows and hurries to the door. Timon tells him to prepare for the worst as he looks back down at the note in his hand and the bird flies away.

"Timon, Your son has been framed murder and Varkas is on his way now to attack your Kingdom. I have stowed away on the flagship with the help of Felligrand but I need your help. Felligrand has told me of a

Crimson sword your son and his allies were talking about as he eavesdropped on one of their conversations. I thought it was only a legend until I saw the books in your son's possession. I am certain now that he is involved in this. Please my friend be safe but prepare for the worst."

I hear someone calling my name. I open my eyes, and see Selph standing over me, telling me it's time to wake up. The smell of fresh air fills my lungs. I look over to my left, and see Tina, sleeping under a bush, with Michie resting on her shoulder fast asleep.

We had been stuck in the tunnel for almost three weeks. Janto grabs my shoulder, and gestures deeper into the tunnel, indicating that we should leave the area. I take a deep breath and stand up. Selph wakes Tina and Michie, and they get to their feet, rubbing sleep from their eyes. We gather up our belongings, and we each take a piece of the dried meat Camilla packed up for us to eat and continue down the road, chewing it slowly. My stomach growls loudly, and I wish we had more to eat.

Janto tells us that we should look for a nearby village. One that's out of the way, and low key enough that the troops won't look for us there. We stop for a moment to take a piss and check the map. After some discussion, we decide to take the route through the mountains, as it's the most inconspicuous. After a few hours of walking, the sun begins to set and we decide it's best to setup camp for the night.

Janto tells Tina and Michie to gather some water for us. Selph and I head into the woods, to find kindling for a fire. While gathering up sticks and logs, I hear a strange noise and as I look around for the source of the sound, I see a huge wild boar. Without any hesitation, I slowly begin to sneak up behind it. Selph spots me sneaking up on the beast, and she crouches down, drawing a knife.

I look over at Selph. She nods at me and she picks up a stone, and strikes it with her knife. A high, clear metallic clang rings out, and the boar looks up, puzzled. When it starts shuffling towards the sound, I pounce on it. I feel something on my back and I fly through the air, landing in a bush close by. My vision spins, and when I regain my senses, I see a huge man standing over me, dressed in a boar skin.

Selph attacks the man from the side, but he calmly extends his hand and she runs straight into it, falling to the ground. The man leans down, picks me up, and hangs me over his shoulders, like I'm nothing more than a rag doll. He begins to make a whining animal noise.

Some Drags appear, each with different color scales from brown, white and red. Their colorful scales and tattered wings glistening beautifully in the sun that shines thru the leaves. along with a Vilfreed, with his slouched posture and black sleek fur shinning brilliantly. In a hushed voice, the Vilfreed announces that there are more people close by and points in the direction of our camp. I try to yell out for Janto, but the man holding me covers my mouth with his hand, and the white scaled Drag grabs Selph while she is lying on the ground, and carries her alongside me.

In the distance, I see our campfire. I hear Janto stand up, and demand to know who's there.
The Drags and the Vilfreed stop, and the man carrying me comes forward throws me to the ground. The Vilfreed walks forward and tells Janto that I attacked his friend. Janto leans down, helps me up, and asks me if this was true and I explain to him that I thought he was a wild boar.

The man behind me lets out a loud bellowing laugh, followed by the

Vilfreed and the rest, including Janto. When they've stopped laughing, the huge man asks if he can join us, and that they would be more than happy to share the food they have caught. Janto smiles and tells them that would be fine.

The Drag with red scales comes forward, and the light from the fire tells me he is a fire Drag, his red scales shimmering brightly next to the flames. As the other one walks over, I see that they are an air and earth Drag. After a while, Michie and Tina return, carrying water in buckets made of Ice that Tina created and everyone introduces themselves.

The person who was carrying me and wearing the boar skin turns out to be a Grunk. Who comes from nomadic mountain dwellers with giant muscles and a pale greenish skin covered in red tribal tattoo's over his body. He tells us he is named Baron, and the Drags introduce themselves as Zil the air drag, Rom the earth drag and Fritz the fire drag. The Vilfreed introduces himself as Ziphone and they ask what our names our. When they get to me, I stay silent, wondering if the troops had put a bounty out on my head.

Baron looks down at me and pats me on the head saying how I must be the strong silent type. I notice Janto staring at me with a look of concern. As we sit by the fire, watching some fresh boar cook over the open fire, they begin to tell us stories of their adventures on the high seas and how they are currently looking for someone. Michie asks who they're looking for and Baron says they're looking for a man named Drac, who murdered the Queen of Arvagi.

A cold chill runs down my spine and I begin to feel clammy. I decide its best to change the subject and I ask Tina why she always uses ice magic over every other element. She lets out a tiny chuckle, saying that it's a silly reason, but Michie begins to goad her, poking her in the side until she admits that she learned ice magic above the other elements, simply so she could sell cold drinks in the tavern instead of warm ones.

Janto lets out a laugh, and Michie soon joins in. Baron asks her why she wears gauntlets as her weapon of choice despite having the ability to freeze things, and she explains that she never learned any combat magic, but being a bartender she learned how to brawl before she learned how to chill a drink.

When the boar is finished cooking, we dig in. The pain in my stomach slowly fades away as I ingest the meat from the wild beast. Baron looks down at me and pulls out a large bottle of hooch from one of his bags and tells us all to drink up. We pass the bottle around the fire all of us sitting, laughing and talking well into the night.

After a while, my eyes begin to grow heavy. Finding a spot underneath a large bush, I wave goodnight to the others and I soon drift off to sleep.

In the morning, I awake to find myself and the others tied up from head to toe. My hands are bound. It's only now that I realize our new companions never had any of the drink they shared with us. As I struggle to get free, I realize the smoldering remains of the campfire are behind me. While they stand around talking, I begin slowly moving towards the remains of the fire, stopping when one of them looks in my direction.

I feel around for any piece of charcoal that's hot enough to burn through the ropes but instead, I find a rock with a sharp corner, which we used to contain the fire. I start cutting into my ropes, as I listen to

Ziphone tell the Drags to get the ship ready for transport. I wonder what he's talking about, as I finish cutting through the ropes around my hands. I suddenly realize that the quickest route back to Arvagi is by ship and there is almost certainly a bounty on my head.

Gritting my teeth, I realize that my sheath and gauntlets have identifying marks that give away my identity. I watch as Ziphone grabs Michie, and and throws him over his shoulder before heading off. I look around, and see Janto and Tina lying on the ground beside me. I hastily reach down towards my boots and begin to cut through the ropes and free myself.

I reach for Janto but before I can start cutting into his ropes, I'm grabbed my Baron. I fight him off, and roll over to a pile of our equipment, grabbing my sword as I do so. Baron tells me to lower my weapon, saying that he's only there to help.

I call him a liar, asking why he tied us up and drugged us if he wasn't looking to hurt us. He lets out a deep sigh, as he stands up, and looks me straight in the eyes.

He charges at me with astounding speed, knocking me down to the ground. I struggle to get a foot hold, and I use my sword to pick myself up. He begins to charge me again, and using this opportunity, I swing at him, striking him on the arm, and I watch as he falls to the ground.

I hobble over towards him, and ask if he's had enough yet and demand that he lets my friends go. I realize at that moment, that his fall was all an act and he grabs my legs and pulls them out from under me.

My head strikes the ground, and my vision blurs from the force of the impact. I try to get back up and fall back down. I feel him grab my boot and begin to drag me back over towards the fire and drop me.

I see a blurred image of him standing over me, holding ropes and I begin to hear Janto come too, asking what has happened to me. As I feel around, I realize my sword is still in my hand so I lash out and lunge towards Baron, thrusting my sword into his chest, feeling the ground shake as he collapses backwards.

Looking down, I see Janto in shock from what happened and he quickly breaks free of his bindings with little effort. He turns to Tina, pulling off her bindings, and shouts at her to wake up and he begins to shake her, telling her that Baron is hurt.

I pull my sword from Baron's chest, while he gags on his own blood. Tina and Janto run to his side. I tell them that they should leave him, that he got what he deserved. As I turn and walk away, I see Janto's fist coming towards me. His punch sends me flying through the air, and I land a few feet away, holding my face.

He looks down at me, and calls me a fool, telling me that Baron and his friends were looking for us so that they could help us escape and if I had bothered to listen, I would've known like everyone else.

I yell back at Janto, demanding to know how I could have known. He ignores me, and turns to Tina and begins to instruct her on how to cast a simple fire spell to cauterize Baron's wounds before he bleeds out.

Watching as Ziphone and the rest arrive to try and help Baron, and I stand back and realize that he may be dying because of me. I wasn't able to see the signs that everyone else did. Because of my mistake, an innocent life may fade from this world.

I walk away, and collect my sheath and equipment, while everyone else is distracted by Baron and I head off into the woods, leaving everyone behind. I tell myself that if I stay with them, they will only get hurt and that it's better off this way.

Night soon falls, and I look around for some shelter. I decide to keep walking, as I see nowhere good to set up camp. I stumble in the dark and wish that my sheath would light the way for me, for some reason it remains dark.

I think of Baron, and how he's probably dead by now because of me, and the thought of it makes my gut wrench in pain. As I continue down the road, the sun begins to appear over the horizon and the path begins to light up before me.

As I continue walking, I begin to feel tiredness creeping up on me. A loud scream echoes through the woods. I rush down the path as fast as I can, and see a woman with blonde hair being attacked by a wild Vilfreed. I run towards her and pick up a pebble from the ground.

Throwing the pebble at him, he turns, his red eyes glaring at me through the darkness. It crouches, poised to pounce, and dig into me with its sharp teeth and I draw my sword. He begins to charge at me. Its claws rip into my left arm, and thinking fast, I wrap my arm around him and hold him close to me and before his other claws have a chance to cut into me, I thrust my sword through its chest.

Kicking him away, I look around and see three more Vilfreeds coming towards me. I feel a sharp pain in my back. Turning around, I see a fourth Vilfreed staring at me and in that moment I'm overcome with rage.

Grabbing the one behind me by the jaw, I tear him in half with my sword. It falls to the ground, howling in pain. I turn back around and charge at the two of the Vilfreeds, and I swing down with my sword and cleave them both in two.

Looking over to my right, I see the last Vilfreed bearing down on the girl, and I walk towards them. I can see the terror in its eyes grow with east step I take. It falls backwards onto the ground, scratching away at the dirt as it pushes itself away and I grab it by its throat and lift it into the air.

It suddenly thrusts forward with impossible speed, and I feel the claws raking through my skin like knives. I cough, and feel blood trickling from the corner of my mouth. I grasp my sword tightly in my hand and drive it into the beast's chest over and over again. It struggles to scream, and I throw him to the ground, dead like all the others.

I look down at my body, and blood spreading across my front and for a brief moment, I think I see the Crimson sword in my hand. I look over at the girl and ask if she is alright, but before I can finish asking my strength leaves me and I collapse to the ground.

As the world around me fades to black, I hear her let out another scream and I hear two people come running over towards me. I don't know where I am anymore. All I see is darkness. The world around me has vanished, and all I see is an abyss, void of all life. I hear a laugh echoing through the abyss one that sounds like it's filled with cruelty.

When I wake up, I find myself lying in bed, with a fire roaring next to me, in the middle of a small shack.
Looking around, I can see two elderly people, a man and a woman, laying up against the wall sleeping with their heads together, wearing nothing but old tattered clothes. I see the girl from before asleep near the bed, holding my shirt in one of her hands and a sewing needle in the other.

I lie back down in the bed. The blonde girl stirs, yawning as she does so. She sits up, wiping the sleep from her eyes, and smiles at me. She thanks me for saving her from the wild Vilfreeds that attacked her and hands me my shirt back. She informs me that I've lost a lot of blood and that I need to rest.

As if to agree with her, I feel a sharp stabbing pain in my left arm. She looks at me, puts one of her hands gently onto my back, and one onto my chest and helps me lay down. I begin to grow drowsy once more and I watch as she moves over towards my pillow and lays down closer to me and whispers into my ear telling me that if I need anything that she will be right here next to me. As her words echo through my mind, I feel my eyes getting heavy and almost immediately, I drop off into a sound sleep.

The next morning, I get out of bed and wander outside. I look around for the bodies of the Vilfreeds I killed but I don't see any. I turn to the girl and asked her what happened to them and she tells me that I a few weeks have passed since I killed them and that her father has since burned the bodies, to keep unwanted predators away.

I hobble around their tiny home, and she walks by my side. She asks me what my name is and I tell her that it's Drac. She grabs me, looks into my eyes as I look into her blue eyes and she asks me if I am the wanted Prince on all the posters in town.

Gritting my teeth, I decide it's best to lie to her but before I can she tells me that she has known for a while - the Insignia on all my equipment is that of the Kingdom of Zarian. I feel like an idiot. I really should try to scratch all those symbols off.

Just then, the older man approaches us. He introduces himself as Tro Willford, and he introduces the girl as Estra Willford, his daughter. She does a small curtsy, with her old tattered dress, smiling charmingly. The older woman joins us, and introduces herself as Esteem Wilford. She thanks me for rescuing her daughter from the Vilfreeds, and tells me I can stay as long as I need.

I tell them that it would be a bad idea for me to stay in one place for too long, as it might bring unwanted trouble their way, and they look at me with sad expressions. Estra asks me if I would at least stay for a few more days, to make sure I'm fully healed, and I tell her yes. She smiles happily, and her parents go back to working in the garden.

I head back inside and lie back down on the bed and look up at the ceiling. After a while her father comes in, asking me if I know what's going on with the world. He tells me that the Vilfreeds have never attacked people at random before and that the ones I killed had acted as if possessed.

I explain to him that I cannot give no solid answers as to why these things have happened. He asks if Estra can come with me when I leave. He explains that he is incapable of fighting anymore and that it is not safe here anymore.

He begs and pleads, asking me to take Estra with me, and I explain to him that it isn't safe to travel with me. He tells me that he understands my trepidation, but at least with me, she would have a chance at living.

His words echo in my mind as he leaves the room. Asking me to at least think about it. Laying in bed, I go back to staring at the ceiling, and all I can think about is her.

I close my eyes for a moment and when I open them, the sun has already set. Estra comes over carrying a bowl of potato stew, which she fills from a cauldron suspended over the fire. As she hands me the bowl, I ask why it's only potatoes in water, with no meat or milk. Her father stops eating, and tells me that they only pretend it's a stew, because of how poor they are. Estra turns back to me and tells me not to worry about it and that someday things will change.

Smiling, I take a spoonful of potato stew and begin to eat. Estra smiles at me, and she turns back around. After dinner, her parents take the dishes outside to wash them. Estra begins to change my bandages. She asks me how I got the scar on my stomach, and I tell her that a friend gave his life to save mine and that it is a reminder.

She stops for a moment and starts grinding some herbs in a pestle and mortar, to make a salve for my wounds. She tells me to lay back down on the bed so she can apply the medicine. I look towards the wall, as she massages the salve into my wounds. A cool, calming feeling begins to ease the pain away, as Estra tells me how thankful she is to have met me that day, and how sad she will be when I leave.

I begin to drift off to sleep. The next morning, I wake up to find Estra asleep by my side, with her head resting on the side of the bed. I get up from the bed, making sure I don't wake her, and put on my tunic and head outside.

I see her father working in the tiny field next to the house, and her mother doing some gardening and I walk over to tell him that I will be leaving today. He stops, lowers his tools, and without turning to face me, he accepts. He thanks me again for saving his daughter and I tell him it was nothing.

As he goes back to working the field, I tell him I will allow Estra to come with me and I see the glimmer of tears rolling down his cheek. He thanks me, and asks when we will be leaving. I tell him that it will most likely be in a few hours, and he nods his head and goes back to working the field.

Walking over to her mother, I carefully bend over and help her pick herbs from the garden and plant some carrots. I tell her that her daughter is welcome to come with me when I leave today, and she thanks me. Estra soon walks out from the building, wiping sleep from her eyes, and asks what we are talking about.

Her father walks over to us, and explains that she will be coming with me when I leave today. Estra thinks it's a joke at first, but then realizes that her parents are being serious. They explain to her that they don't have the strength to protect her anymore like they did when they were younger. I listen as they argue and how Estra wants to stay with them and I interrupt them.

I ask Estra to stay by my side. She blushes as I explain to her that I need someone with me as I go on my journey. I see her parents' with tears now streaming down their cheeks, begging her to go with me and as I look back over to her, Estra tells them that she will go with me. Her parents wrap their arms around her and tell her just how much they love her.

Chapter Seven

War

It's not long before we start preparing to leave. I pick up my satchel and gauntlets, and put them on while Estra packs her meager belongings into a small bag of her own. I watch as Esteem packs her clothes. Estra glances across at me, and smiles. She walks towards me, and then pushes me onto the bed. When I look puzzled by her behavior, she just laughs, kneels down, and slides her slender arms under the bed. A moment later, she pulls out a heavy looking chest appears, scraping loudly against the hard wood of the floor.

I climb off the bed and help her slide it out. Pulling on the chest, I struggle to move it. Estra is stronger than she looks, and she flushes slightly as she does more of the work than I do. I wish Tina or Janto were here. At the tavern, I had seen Tina lugging around full barrels of mead like they were little more than paperweights.

Estra unclips the latches, and flips open the lid, grunting slightly with the effort. I don't know what expect to see when she opens the chest, but I expect it to be something heavy – perhaps armor, or a secret stash of gold that she had been saving for a rainy day. But when she opens it, I'm surprised to see nothing of any weight at all. The chest itself was made of a thick, dark oak, and I suppose that's where the weight actually comes from. All that Estra pulls from the chest is a long, stunning dress. I turn away, and stare at the wall as Estra changes. As I hear her clothes hit the floor, I catch a glimpse of her reflected in the window. I quickly shut my eyes, to preserve her modesty.

A moment later, she declares herself ready, and I turn back around. She has her arms aloft, and a radiant smile spread across her lips, and as she spins around, the dress whips outwards, revealing shapely, toned calf muscles. She smiles, as I look her up and down, and then she curtseys,

Her mother and father enter, smiling proudly at their little girl, now a grown up, ready to leave on an adventure into the big wide world. Their smiles mask their tears, and it's obvious they're just putting on a brave face – her mother's eyes have the slight shine that only shows when someone is holding back a torrent of tears. They stand together arm in arm, and hug their daughter, and kiss her goodbye. Not wanting to intrude on this family moment, I leave the room, and wait outside.

A minute or so later, the door opens, and Estra walks out, her own eyes misty with tears. She's clutching her bag and a walking stick her father always used. Her father follows her out, and he places a hand on my shoulder before we leave.

"Forgive my wife for not coming out to say goodbye to you properly Drac. Saying goodbye to her child has hit her rather hard, and I'm afraid she's not in the right frame of mind to focus on manners at this moment." I tell him not to worry about it, and he smiles, and shakes me by the hand. Estra takes me by the arm, and holds me close.

"Father, don't worry about me. I have my very own noble, handsome prince to protect me. Who knows perhaps one day I'll become a princess." She says one more heartfelt goodbye, and tells her father to say goodbye to her mother one last time, and then we're gone, walking down the dirt track leading away from the house. Looking back, I can see Tro waving, and he stays there, watching us go, until we've turned a corner and he's gone out of sight.

She takes my arm as we walk and for an hour or so, as we walk in this fashion. I ask her about the dress, and she tells me that it's a treasured heirloom, and the most valuable thing she owns. Frowning, I ask her why she is wearing such a beautiful dress for such menial labor as hiking through a wood. She smiles and tells me that she isn't worried about getting it dirty.

"I've never worn it for anything. Never been invited to a ball. Never been to an exquisite banquet. Never danced the night away with lords and princes and all the other noblemen. I don't want to die without ever getting a chance to wear this dress. If I ruin it, hiking through a muddy field, I'm sure I'll regret it, when I'm an old woman looking back on my life from an old dusty armchair. But for now, I just want to wear it, and look the best I'll ever look, and if I die on the road, I'll look back with no regrets knowing I got to wear the dress I love so much.

I hold her close, and tell her that, had she lived near my castle, she would have been invited to all the parties, peasant or not. No sooner have these words left my lips, before a rustling in the bushes startles me. Estra gets behind me, and I place my hand on the hilt of my sword, ready to draw the moment I see the whites of our assailant's eyes.

"Who's there?" I shout, trying not to let my voice waver as I speak. "Show yourself!"

The bushes rustle once more and Selph steps out from behind the trees, looking at me with a look of anger on her face that could melt steel. A gust of wind flows down on us, and with a boom, Zil lands before us, wings spread wide, nostrils flared, no trace of a smile on his face.

My friends are furious with me, and I don't blame them. I turn to Estra, who's holding me so close to her body that I can feel her breasts pressed against my back. I whisper in her ear not to worry, and as I look over her shoulder, I see Janto approaching us from behind. Breaking free from Estra's tight grip, I walk towards him, eyes fixed on his, trying to paste the most confident look can muster onto my face.

When we meet, I look him in the eye. My lips tighten involuntarily, as I try to resist the urge to shake and cry. He regards me coolly, and there's a dead silence between us, as the seconds tick by. I finally open my mouth, but when I try to speak, no sound comes out, and my lip starts to shake. I try again, and all that comes out is a dry croak. I clear my throat, and open my mouth once more, but before I can finally speak, a booming voice stops me.

"Drac! Come with me if you want to live!"

I turn my neck slowly, breaking eye contact with Janto, and look into the trees beside me. I hear sticks crunch, as a huge man steps out from behind a tree. I look into his eyes, and Baron looks back into mine, a smile crossing his lips.

He laughs and asks me why I'm beaten to hell, and covered in bandages. I stare at him wordlessly, unable to speak. Baron lets out another laugh.

"How?..." I ask, stunned to see the huge man standing before me, when I assumed him to be dead.

I hear the rumbling of feet drumming against the dirt path, and I look around confused. Janto curses grabs me, and drags me into the bushes. Estra is left standing on the path, confused, and frozen with fear. Selph grabs her arm, and pulls her into the bushes next to us, as the rumbling grows louder.

I open my mouth to ask what's going on, and Janto shushes me, with his finger pressed against his lips. We all hold our breath and freeze, as the thundering footsteps reach draw nearer and nearer. Troops storm past, a full platoon, with heavy armor, and enormous weapons strapped to their belts. They're elite soldiers, terrifyingly strong, and armed to the teeth.

As the last troop passes, we climb out of the bushes. Estra has a look of utter terror on her face, and she's gripping Selph's arm so tightly that Selph is wincing in pain. I gently pry Estra away from Selph, and she grabs my body and presses herself against me. Rubbing her arm, Selph looks across at the new girl, with a strange look on her face. I'm not sure, but I think I detect a note of envy on her pretty eyes, and I try to smile at her. She simply turns away, nose upturned, chest puffed out proudly.

Once Estra has calmed down, I crouch, and look at the tracks left behind by the platoon of soldiers. The hard dirt track shouldn't preserve much of a print when a foot lands on it, but these troops have left clear markings. Each footstep is deep, and I can tell from looking at them that each troop must be incredibly heavy. With such heavy equipment, there was no way they should be able to move so quickly – and yet, I have just witnessed it with my own two eyes. These soldiers are simply inhuman. I almost don't believe such men can exist.

Janto nudges me in the side, and tells me we need to get moving. I stand up, and follow him into the woods, leaving the path behind us. As we head into the dense trees, Estra sticks close to me, and I quietly tell her about my friends, who they are and how I came to meet them. The others don't seem interested in the strange newcomer who has joined us on our journey. Selph is particularly distant, walking apart from the rest of the group, eyes fixed in front of her, each step driven with a furious energy that I don't quite understand. I leave her alone, and let her walk on her own.

As we move deeper into the forest, I hear the faint sound of moving water. The trees start thinning, and we reach a clearing with a river meandering through it. A boat is moored there, with the Argavi flag hanging limply from the mast. Tina and Michie are on the deck, Michie waving at me as he sees me approaching. Tina looks dramatically less happy to see me.

A shadow spreads around us, accompanied by the sound of powerful wings cutting through the air. We look up, as Zil descends, with a panicked expression on his snouted face.

"More troops are on their way!" he shouts, as he lands on the soft grass besides us. Baron leaps onto the boat. I hear a crunch, and Tina winces – the deck has splintered beneath his enormous weight, although the damage seems to have been confined to a single plank of wood. I glance at Estra, as she nervously studies Zil. I give her arm a reassuring squeeze, and she smiles at me, although she does move around me, so my body is between her and the Drag.

We climb aboard the boat – I go to help Estra, but she leaps across without any trouble at all. The cabin door opens, and out steps Felligrand. He looks across to me, gives a quick wink to me, and then becomes all business. He gives the order to lift the anchor, as I see troops appearing from beneath the trees, drawing bows from their backs. Janto yells at us to get down, and I grab Estra and pull her down to the floor of the deck beside me. I cover her with my body, as arrows fly over our heads. I feel her chest rise and fall beneath mine, as she lays there underneath me, and I take her hand, trying to gently calm her.

There's a loud crash, and I glance up. Fritz has fallen, am arrow protruding from his scaly arm. I feel the boat start to move, and I hear the voices of the soldiers, yelling to one another. More and more arrows fly overhead, as they desperately try to halt our escape. Some of them sink deep into the mast, biting into the surface of the wood with a splintering crunch. We stay down, and wait for the hail of arrows to die down.

We slowly get back up, and look out over the side of the boat. The soldiers are little more than dots in the distance. They're attempting to make chase, but they're not making much headway closing the distance. Tina is trying to treat Fritz's wounded arm, and his yelps of pain are like a knife being plunged into my eardrums. Estra runs over, and asks to see the wound. The arrowhead has buried itself deep in his arm, and his blood has started to clot around it. He digs his claws into the deck of the ship, and Estra pulls it from his arm.

I watch as she opens her satchel and begins to make a paste for the wound. She daubs the wound with the paste, and massages it gently. As she rubs the paste into the injury, Fritz's yelps begin to subside. She bandages him up, and helps him back to his feet. Fritz thanks her, and the other drags are quick to thank her as well. She just smiles nonchalantly, and says it was nothing.

They begin to discuss her knowledge of medicine and healing. I'm listening in as Janto walks over to me, to ask where I've been for the past few weeks. I regale him with the story of what happened after my fight with Baron and how I met Estra and her family when she was attacked by a group of wild Vilfreeds.

Ziphone overhears my story and comes over to join us. He asks about the Vilfreeds and I list everything I remember about them. He turns away, and has a hushed conversation with Felligrand. I can't make out what they're saying, but their faces are urgent and tense. Felligrand nods in agreement, and gestures to Zil, who flaps his wings, and soars up into the air. We watch as he hovers above the ship, and begins flapping his wings vigorously in the direction of the ship. The wind created by his flapping wings pushes the ship forward, and we fly forward with a sudden burst of speed.

Felligrand has taken control of the ship's wheel, and he's carefully guiding us down the river, following the winding path the river wove through the woods. I head over to him, and ask him why he's here. He explains that as well as being a Captain in the Arvagi navy, he's also a smuggler on the side.

Felligrand reveals that he was hired by my father, to come and retrieve me, after word reached him that I had been framed for murder. Felligrand sees the look of shock upon my face and tells me not to worry.

Janto comes over, and asks how my father had come to hear about the murder. Felligrand says he doesn't know, but he was happy to be hired for a dishonest day's work, transporting us across the ocean back to the Kingdom of Zarian.

Felligrand tells us that he needs the deck mopped and the cargo hold organized to make enough space to accommodate everyone. With the injuries Baron and Fritz sustained, it would be hard for them to help out. I feel guilty knowing that I was the one who injured Baron, and so I tell him that I'll get straight to work. I head down into the hold to help out.

There are two sets of stairs leading down and Fritz pops up telling me to join him from the left one. Down in the hull, I see Baron sitting in the back, resting against the cabin wall, snoring loudly. Fritz asks me if I want to play a game of Teos and I explain to him that I don't know the rules.

We sit on either side of a table, and he tries to teach me the game. After half an hour or so, Baron wakes up, and tells Fritz that he should give up teaching me the game because it won't catch on. I hear footsteps coming down the stairs and Janto walks into the room. I think he's going to be angry at me for shirking off my work, but when he sees the game of Teos, he lets out a laugh and sits down, telling me to watch. After a while, Fritz begins to complain that Janto is cheating. I ask Janto how he managed to win so easily. He explains to us that my father plays all the time back at home, and they've been playing together for many years.

I'm puzzled by this - I never took my father for the game playing type. I almost always saw him with Borus talking about politics. I ask Janto if Borus plays the game as well and he lets out a laugh, and tells us that he invented the game and taught it to them.

Fritz storms off, angered that Janto had had such an unfair advantage. Baron chuckles, and tells us not to worry about it. Being a fire drag, Fritz has always been a hot head.

Baron asks me what I'm doing down in the hull and I explain to him that I came to help them organize the cargo hold. He tells me not to worry about it - Grunks heal fast.

Baron and Janto head back up the stairs to the deck of the ship to see if any work needs doing leaving me below and I think on what he said.

A month has passed since we set out from the Kingdom of Arvagi, when a mass of Arvagi ships appears on the horizon. We're not far off the coast of the Zarian Kingdom, and King Timon, clad in his finest clothes, watching from his throne room through the window overlooking the ocean. He turns to Borus and tells him to call for Ignkeal and ready for battle.

Borus leaves the room and for a short while Timon stares out at the sea, clenching his fist in anger. A loud roar echoes from overhead and the room shakes as Ignkeal lands on the balcony before him. Borus returns to the throne room and walks out onto the balcony, carrying a tanned leather saddle, and attaches to two golden chains from Ignkeal to it. Timon following him out, tells him to prepare for the worst, before climbing into the saddle on Ignkeal.

Letting out a mighty roar that shakes the castle, Ignkeal spreads his wings and begins to ascend. They head out to sea, heading for the flagship of the Arvagi Kingdom.

Watching the King leave, Borus hastily makes his way to the catacombs and begins to descend into darkness. The stairs look much the same as they did when Drac had gone down these stairs all those months ago, except strange letters and markings are now glowing from the walls. Borus reaches the room where the sword of Zara was waiting for Drac.

A short while later, Timon descends onto the deck of the Arvagi Kingdom's flagship. The weight of the dragon pushes the boat downwards into the water, the deck creaking beneath him. The King dismounts his steed, which flies back up into the sky so that the ship isn't weighed down. Soon, the soldiers of Arvagi begin to surround him.

The soldiers point their spears at Timon, who demands to know who's in charge. Looking over to the Captain's quarters. The doors swing open and Varkus appears before him, wearing a regal crimson tunic, with a black trim. He laughs as he approaches Timon, who's being restrained by the soldiers. Thick ropes are produced, and roughly secured around Timon's wrists and ankles, binding his hands behind his back.

"Drac has committed treason against the throne. He murdered Triemeith, the Queen of Arvagi and now his life is forfeit." A boot hits Timon's knee, knocking him down. He looks up at Varkus, from his hands and knees, who cackles madly. One of the soldiers kicks him in the stomach, and the impact knocks the wind out of him. Gasping for air, the King demands proof of his son's wrongdoings.

Varkus laughs, and turns away for a moment, heading back down the stairs into the bowels of the ship. He reappears moments later, holding a sword. Timon looks up at the familiar blade: It's Drac's sword. Varkus throws it to the ground before the King, and looks at the King's face, laughing as he does so. Varkus kneels down next to the King, as he struggles against his bonds. The soldiers laugh cruelly, and stab at him with their spears, harshly enough to draw blood, but not so hard as to risk killing their captive.

"You recognize this weapon, do you not? It was pulled straight from Triemeith's chest." Varkus demands. The King nods weakly.

"Yes... It's Drac's blade."

Varkus smiles, his thin lips twisted into a smirk, and rises back to his feet. He paces back and forth in front of Timon, and explains that by such a treasonous act he has declared war on the entire kingdom of Arvagi. The only way to atone for such a heinous crime is to put an end to the kingdom of Zarian.

"No-one of your tainted bloodline will ever seize power again. We will rip your family right out of history, and Arvagi will lead this world into endless prosperity." Varkus turns to the soldiers, and takes a spear from one of them.

"I have enjoyed our chat, Timon. It is a shame to dirty the deck of this beautiful boat with your sour blood. Alas, it is as it must be. I shall end you here and now. Then I will track down your son, and end him. And once your pathetic family are dead, I will take your heads, stick them on pikes, and then we will slay everyone in your entire kingdom." Varkus savors every single word, as if he is drinking a fine wine. "Well, perhaps not everyone. I think there might be a place aboard our ship for some of your prettier women. It's a long journey, sailing back to Arvagi, and my men will need something to entertain them on the way home."

The men raise their spears, and roar like savages. Many start shouting their praises, desperate to be noticed by their new lord – there are shouts of "Hail, King Varkus, first of his name," and "Lord of the Realm, lead us to prosperity." Varkus smiles, arrogance leaking from his every feature, as he raises the spear in his hands, and points it at Timon's heart. The defeated King closes his eyes, and stares fiercely at Varkus.

The spear clatters to the floor as the evil King looks down on Timon, Silent laughter burns from his eyes, and he raises a hand to silence the circle of jeering soldiers.

"Slaying the King with an Arvagi spear would be easy, would it not? But wouldn't it be poetic, if I were to finish him with a weapon of some significance to him. Yes, I think justice would be done if I were to slay the father with say, his own son's blade."

The men cheer once more, and laugh wildly. One steps forward and takes back his spear from the ground, as Varkus picks up Drac's sword and balances it in his hands, testing its edge with his thumb. He points the sword at Timon's heart. As Timon continues to stare fiercely, Varkus whispers to him, his voices dripping with mock sympathy.

"Do not be afraid Timon. Look on the bright side – I'll make sure my men give you a dignified sendoff. Will a burial at sea be all right with you? I'm afraid that's all we'll be able to offer. Well, I call it a burial at sea. We'll dump your body overboard, and watch you sink. I'll be sure to take your crown though. A King is nothing without a crown."

He pulls the sword back, but just as he prepares to plunge the sword into the King's chest, a female voice rings out across the deck. The soldier's look around in a panic trying to figure out where the voice came from as bats descend from the sky and begin flapping around the entrance of the Captain's quarters. They form a whirling pyramid of darkness, and when they scatter, they reveal a woman, clad in tightly bound black leather, a look of fury on her face.

Varkus falls down in shock, dropping the sword of Zara in shock. He begins to push himself away from her as she walks towards him. The soldiers begin to back away, as Varkus cries out to them, demanding they kill her. When the woman steps out of the shadows, into the sunlight, smoke begins to rise from her skin, and the King sees her face.

"Triemeith."

The soldiers begin to leap overboard in terror, begging her not to kill them. Varkus struggles to his feet, and asks her how she's still alive. In a flash, Triemeith vanishes. Varkus looks around, wide eyed with fear. For a moment, he rests, chest rising and falling in rapid breaths. An unnatural calmness fills the air for a moment. The stillness is pierced by a Varkus's terrified scream, as a slim, feminine hand appears on his shoulder. With inhuman strength, the hand spins him around, bringing him face to face with the beautiful rage of Triemeith's crimson eyes. He rips himself away, and runs as fast as he can. Timon reaches out and grabs his ankle, bringing him crashing to the ground.

Timon rises to his feet, and looks down at the pitiful Varkus cowering at his feet.

"Did you think you had killed the Queen, you fool? How can you kill someone who's already dead?" he steps forward, and picks up the Sword of Zara from the deck. "Triemeith died many years ago. I was there. I bore witness to her resurrection."

He points the sword at Varkus, who places his hands over his head, and winces in fear.

"She is undead, Varkus. Bound to the mortal realm by a force that no mere mortal can understand. And now you too will bear witness to a resurrection of sorts. The Queen looks hungry! You will serve as an excellent source of fuel for her."

Varkus stares at Triemeith looming over him. Her eyes are glowing blood red and fixed on him. She smiles, revealing savage fangs, as two gigantic black wings emerge from her back covering all three of them in shadow.

Varkus screams and tries to claw himself away, but it's too late. The shadows that extend over him holds him in place, and she grabs him by the ankle. His fingernails leave scrape marks in the deck as she drags him towards her. Triemeith closes her wings around him, and there is a sickening squelching sound. For a few moments Triemeith and Varkus are both hidden from view, behind the great wings of shadow, and then the wings spread once more. Her body is now covered in grotesque muscles, which bulge and shift beneath her skin, as if they're made out of live snakes. Raw energy radiates from her entire body, and the pressure is flowing through the air in waves.

She drops the remains of Varkus's body to the floor. It's been stripped of all fluids and life, a wrinkled husk of its former self. She flings her head back, and screams. The energy flows from her body, and flies free, in bursts of black lightning. Her body settles, and reduces and in the blink of an eye, she returns to her former self once more.

Timon turns away, and looks down at the sword of Zara.

"How can that sword be here? I gave it to one of my maids to return to Drac." Triemeith asks him.

"I believe the sword you returned to Drac to be a fake." Timon replies. "He is most likely in danger. Will you join me in the coming battle?"

"Yes Timon. My troops will be ready to join the fight, and together we will end the chaos that's taken over the land."

She reaches over and places her hand onto his back and holds him close, and they stare off over the rolling ocean, towards the Kingdom of Zarian.

"Timon" she asks in a calming voice, "Why did you not tell Janto and the rest that I am undead, or that I am the Queen of Arvagi?"

"Alas, my lady. I couldn't bear to hurt my friends. Can you imagine the pain of being told that one you loved is now among the undead?"

Silence falls between them, and for a moment they stand and look out over the bow, simply examining Zarian. For now, it was quiet and peaceful, but that would not last much longer. Timon wishes he could stay a while and talk with Triemeith – after all these years, it is good to see her once again, even if she is no longer entirely human.

He turns away from her, and heads to the helm of the ship. There's no time for pleasantries at this time.

War is coming, and it's time for action.

Chapter Eight

Seal

Off in the distance, I can see the castle. We docked back in Zarian only an hour ago, and from that moment we hadn't stopped running. Janto is running beside me, with a determined glint in his eyes. To my left, Estra is running as fast as her legs can carry her. She looks exhausted, but she hasn't stopped or complained yet. Looking back out across the ocean, I can make out Arvagi ships docking and the soldiers beginning to row towards land. The others are racing along behind us, with the exception of Zil, who's flying overhead.

When we reach the crest of the hill, Selph tells us she's going to go on ahead and warn my father about the incoming attack on the castle. Janto tells her to hurry, and she darts by all of us, with impressive speed. Just as she disappears from view over the dip of the hill, the ground begins to shake beneath my feet. At first it's a gentle tremor, but it builds into a huge rumble. It feels as though the earth is going to open and swallow us whole. Estra grabs my hand to try and keep me from falling down.

"What's going on?" Michie screams, Tina gripping his arm tightly.

We're all at a loss for words. Zil lands beside us, trying to help, but landing back on the shaking earth nearly throws him straight off his feet. I hear a scream of pain, and I turn to see Ziphone down on all fours, screeching in pain. Fritz crouches beside him, shaking him, and asking if he's alright. Ziphone lets out another scream, and we all feel the piercing cold of the demonic pressure emanating from the castle.

We watch on in horror as Ziphone screams over and over, unable to keep his own body under control. He rolls over, arms flailing wildly. He stops on his back, and screeches like a demon. He stops moving, and stays dead still. The ground stops shaking, as suddenly as it began. Everyone is frozen in a stunned silence.

I hear Estra gasp beside me and my eyes snap open. For a moment, my mind refuses to believe what I'm seeing before me.

Ziphone has sat up, eyes glowing demonic red. Fritz is staring at him, mouth agape. In one fell movement, Ziphone raises a claw, and plunges it straight through Fritz's chest. The claws go straight through his body, punching a hole right through him. I reach out toward him, but Felligrand pushes me back, telling me to run.

I grab Estra's hand and we begin to sprint toward the castle. Janto, Michie and Tina follow behind us. My head is bowed and there are tears in my eyes. I see Selph running towards me, with Borus hot on her heels. Selph must have moved really fast to have reached the castle so quickly.

Borus rushes over to me, but before I can say a word, he spins me around, and takes the Sword of Zara from my back.

"Do you know what this is Drac?" he bellows in my face, brandishing the sword with a withered old hand. I can feel Estra's hands on my tunic, cowering behind me. Borus begins mutter under his breath. I can't make out his words, but they seem to be having an effect on the sword – it's begins to shine with its usual blue light.

The sword begins to glitter. Sparks fly as though a whetstone is being scraped across the blade at a ferocious tempo. There's an angry hissing sound, and an echoing screech that sounds like it's coming from a million miles away, even though it's coming from right in front of me.

We all watch on in horror as the teal sword and letters begin to burn with a red flame. The flame spreads across the blade, and the metal begins to change. At first the changes are subtle, and then they begin to become more pronounced. Borus staggers backwards, dropping the sword to the ground, and falls back, with a look of shock on his face.

The sword stops screeching, and settles down. I stare at it, stunned – it's the crimson sword that hosted Apocalypse for all that time. But if this is this the crimson sword, then where's the real Sword of Zara? No sooner had the question come into my mind, than I had the answer. It was taken from me at the castle. The wrong sword had been returned to me, magically disguised as my own sword.

"It's all over!" Borus exclaims, his voice little more than a harsh, desperate whisper.

"Drac, what's going on?" Estra's hand grips my forearm like a vice as she cries out in fear.

Borus looks up at us, looking older than I've ever seen him look. He explains to us that if the crimson sword ever came this close to the castle, then the creature that had been sealed away by my ancestors would awaken.

"I was one of the few immortals from that time. I stayed behind when they departed this world, to ensure peace and safety remained after the War of Heaven's Fall was over." He looks as though he is about to cry.

I should have known he was telling the truth about his age when we talked all that time ago, but I didn't think much of it at the time. I ask him what we can do to stop the revival of Apocalypse.

"Nothing... There's nothing we can do." He stops for a moment and asks me how I know the name of the creature. I pull the book we found back in Arvagi's library from my satchel and hand it to him.

He begins to furiously rifle through the pages, until he finds a passage near the back. He looks up at us and tells us there may still be a chance to save the day. He explains to us that if we can lure him into the room from which I got the sword of Zara, there may be a chance to create a new seal similar to the one that my ancestors used to place his soul into the sword.

I ask him if there is any other way. Borus looks at us with a great sadness in his eyes and tells us that there isn't and if Apocalypse isn't sealed back up then it may be not only the end of the Kingdom, but the end of the entire world.

I turn to Estra and tell her to stay with Selph. She looks into my eyes, tells me to come back safe, and kisses me on the cheek. Janto grabs my shoulder, and tells me we've got to go. I look back at Estra one final time, and then turn away.

Borus hands the book back to me. We look towards the castle, knowing this may be the last fight we face together.

We leave Estra and Selph at the base of the hill, and head off to the castle. It's a short walk, and when we arrive at the gates, I hear the sound of Ignkeal landing behind us. I turn to see my father dismounting the dragon. Borus stops beside him, and they speak to each other about something. They're too far away for me to make out precisely what. I'm about to head back and speak to him, when Janto grabs me once more, and tells me there's no time.

I wish that I had had time to say a proper goodbye to my father, Selph and Estra. We head into the castle garden, and begin to descend down the stairs. For a brief moment, I feel something tugging on the back of my shirt but I ignore it as we reach the entrance of the garden. The sky has changed from its usual beautiful blue to a shocking blood red. The ground begins to shake under our feet once more.

We venture outside, past the blossom trees and to the entrance to the catacombs. Janto leads us, and lights a torch as he and leads us down the stairwell. As we reach the black door that was once bolted shut, we see that it's since been torn open and we begin to hear a gasping sound as if someone is trying to breathe.

When we reach the bottom of the stairs, we find a suit of black armor. The Crimson sword leaps out of my hands, and lands in the hands of the black armor. Fear grips our hearts as the suit begins to morph, softening, until it changes from metal to flesh.

It lets out a terrible screech that shakes the room. Dust showers down on us. As we stand there, stricken with terror by the creature, two crimson red eyes begin to appear in the darkness where its helmet was. We watch in horror as the sword illuminates the entire room in a bright crimson red light, revealing his true self to us and for a brief moment we stare at him and he stares back at us.

He leans down, looks me in the eyes, and tells me that he is going to kill me.

I hear Estra's voice, calling out my name, and the sound distracts the monster. It looks over my shoulder, searching for the source of the sound. Estra is stood at the bottom of the stairs, her dress billowing out around her feet. She throws a sword towards me. Her throw is slightly off, but the sword seems to arch through the air, bending towards me, as if it has a mind of its own. It lands in the palm of my hand and I grip it tightly. Shock fills the creature's face as I grasp the handle of the sword, and I see that it's the Sword of Zara. I roll to the side, breaking free of the monster's clutches, and rise to my feet brandishing the sword before me.

He lets out a roar and the room begins to shake once more. I run, the others following me towards the room where months ago, I received the Sword of Zara. The monster vanishes, and we're glad to be rid of the monster. We reach the room, I charge into the centre of the room. I can feel a demonic presence in the room, and I raise the sword as I circle, waiting for the monster to reappear. A scream echoes through the room, I spin around to see that he has appeared by the entrance, holding a struggling Estra in his giant hands.

I look over to Janto. His face says what words never could. There's nothing we can do. We watch on helpless as the creatures grip on Estra begins to tighten. I see the pedestal from which I drew the sword and I know what I must do.

I tell him I'll release his wife as soon as he lets her go. He agrees but warns me that the moment I let her go he is going to kill me. I lift the sword of Zara up and slot it into the pedestal.

The room around us begins to fill with light, as Apocalypse drops Estra to the ground. I run towards her and take her in my arms. She coughs weakly, and places her hand on my cheek. I open my mouth to speak, but no words come out, and for a moment I'm lost looking into her eyes.

"You told me not to come. I should have listened to you," she says, smiling up at me.

"I'd have been killed if you hadn't come to my aid... Estra... I..."

The moment is broken when I feel a sharp tug on my ankle. I fall sideways, and Apocalypse takes hold of me and lifts me into the air.

It feels as though time has slowed to a crawl as he begins to raise his sword. I hear Estra screaming hysterically behind me. As the sword swings toward me, I close my eyes, accepting my fate. I feel a flutter of wind against my cheek, and I open my eyes. Apocalypse has frozen. With a dull groan, he drops me to the ground. I grab Estra and we back up as fast as we can. The creature shakes his head for a moment before charging. He raises his sword as he bears down on me and swings the blade down, but Estra leaps in the way, and he stops mere centimeters from making contact with my head. A few strands of her hair fall to the ground. He takes a few steps back looking at us in shock demanding to know why this is happening.

I hear a female voice clearing her throat, and I look behind me. As if from nowhere, a woman with flowing blonde hair, wearing a white dress has appeared. Her beautiful blue eyes gaze across at Estra and myself, and for some reason, I feel soothed by her smile. She approaches us, still smiling as though nothing untoward is going on. She wraps her arms around us, holding Estra and I close against her body.

She looks over at Apocalypse and tells him that it's alright. We watch as he swings his sword around in the room wildly as if fighting something none of us can see.

My father, Selph and Borus appear in the doorway of the room and the moment the creature notices them, he begins to charge at them, roaring wildly. I redraw the sword from the pedestal and rush towards Apocalypse, leaving Estra, and the mysterious women behind me.

I look across at the others and for a moment, I see everything as a single frame – a still image that sticks in my mind, as clear as crystal. I see my father's tears, rolling down his cheeks. I see Selph reaching out to me, lips parted in a scream of anguish. I see Borus's lined face, desperately trying to hold back the sadness within him.

I slow down, and try to call out to them. The monster is weak. If we just keep fighting, maybe we can slay Apocalypse and put an end to the monster once and for all. They should be drawing their weapons and helping me. Why are they just standing there, looking at me with such sadness in their expressions?

Borus opens his mouth, and for a second, everything becomes still.

"I'm sorry."

And then I realize what they mean to do. They don't have any intention of defeating the beast. They mean to lock it away once more, and if that means locking me, Estra, Janto, Tina and Michie away with it, then so be it. I yell at the others, trying to get them to run. Maybe if I hold the monster off, I can buy them enough time to escape.

"No Drac."

At Janto's voice, I look around. His sword has fallen to the ground before him, and he's knelt down in fealty to my Father. Then I realize he's not bowing to the King. He's bowing to me.

"It's been an honor to serve you my Lord."

The others follow suit, with the exception of Estra and the mysterious woman, who hold their arms out to me, beckoning me to come and join them. My feet carry me over to Estra, and I take her in my arms, and hold her close. Estra begins to hum, a soft sad melody, and I take her hand and take one last look at my faithful band of friends.

And then the doors slam shut and a bright white light engulfs us all. I smile, and give Estra's hand a squeeze, as I feel my heart stop beating.

And from that moment, and feel nothing.

Authors Notes

Drags are a humanoid dragon beings the color of their scales represents the element their race can control. Red representing fire, white representing wind, blue representing water, and green representing nature.

Vilfreeds are humanoid panther like creatures that slouch over and are well-known hunters. However there are some wild ones that do not have the sentience that others in their race have, that lash out and attack others when they are on the hunt.

Grunks are giant pale green monstrous cave dwellers that tattoo themselves with red dyes derived from iron and other minerals they mine. They are generally isolated due to their tribal beliefs but have open trade routes with Kingdoms across the world of Aria.

Amersion is a stone that appeared after the Goddesses left the world of Aria and returned to the Boundless. Just as the relics they left the races of the world seek this precious emerald-green gem for the power it posses. The power to manifest a being's will into power.

Angelics are the Angel's created for the sole purpose of feeding the being by causing strife with the Demonic race. Their bloodline houses nurturing capabilities to heal and to bend elements to their will. Women moreover inherit the Angelic bloodline but in some cases men have been born with it.

Demonics are Demon knights created for the sole purpose of feeding the being by causing strife with the Angelic race. Their bloodline houses the capabilities of overwhelming physical properties such as immense strength, and great speed and armor like skin. Men moreover inherit the Angelic bloodline but in some cases Women have been born with it.

Triodds are three-headed serpents with no legs but do have two arms. They generally inhabit desert regions of the world and love a good argument and are known for bartering about anything at Market stalls and shops.

The Boundless is a realm separated from the mortal realm where the God's and Goddesses dwell for all eternity. The source of infinite knowledge and power. There exists a physical entrance but only those deemed worthy have ever been able to pass into it.

Humans conquered the world thanks to the traits of their Angelic and Demonic bloodlines and with it brought peace and unity among the other races of the world. Kingdoms rose from the strife and fighting they went through ensuring this peace.

Bloodlines is the source of humanities strength whether it be Angelic or Demonic. However the traits they are born with do not encompass all the traits their ancestors had. Everyone human is born with one trait however in very rare cases a person might be born with two or three traits.

Goddesses are beings with infinite power that tied solely to an attribute of their choice regardless if it is Love, Light, or Life. During the creation of the universe they desecrated from the Boundless and brought life to the world of Aria the world that they deemed the chosen planet.